REVOLUTIONARY TALES
FROM TRICKY DICK TO DON THE CON

DAVID SCOTT

Paperback ISBN: 979-8-9881554-0-9

E-Book ISBN: 979-8-9881554-1-6

Table of Contents

21st Century

Tricky Dick

There was a tremendous buzz all over the campus, and a feeling that all hell was about to break loose. Everyone was talking about the student uprisings on college campuses across the country. A student strike at Columbia, caused by the predatory policies of the university toward the Harlem community, shut down the University. Students were protesting the building of a gym on public property that was not accessible to the people who lived in the neighborhood. In Orangeburg, South Carolina, three black students were killed by the State Police for wanting to bowl at a local alley. This was following several nights of peaceful protest at South Carolina State College. This was a few years after the Free Speech movement at Berkley, where students demanded the right to freely express their political beliefs. Groups like the Student Non-Violent Coordinating Committee played an important role in the civil rights movement, and students across the globe were becoming a leading force in the movement to transform society. Like students at many other schools in the country, students at the University of Buffalo wanted to help usher in societal change, as well.

It wasn't like we didn't have lots of issues to complain about. There was the war in Vietnam, from which many of the guys I went to high school with were never returning. There was the second-class treatment of women, and the continuing vestiges of segregation made life difficult, if not impossible, for most Black people.

One night while we were smoking our after-dinner bowl of hashish, my roommates and I were discussing the merits of living in what we thought would be a utopian society.

"If we introduce Socialism here, you'll have to take a pay cut," my roommate, Marty, said.

My other roommate, Sam said. "We might be wasting our time going to college if we're going to make the same money practicing law as digging ditches. We might be better off saving our tuition and buying better weed."

I didn't agree with dropping out of school, but had no problem with buying better weed.

"That's not the way socialist societies work," I told them. "People earn based on what they do. Lawyers don't get paid the same as ditch diggers. They just don't become multi-millionaires."

It was October, and Hubert Humphrey was running for President against Richard Nixon, who we affectionately called Tricky Dick. As a bad option for those people wanting to bring back slavery, a third candidate was running named George Corley Wallace. He governed Alabama with the permission of the Ku Klux Klan, and the only rights he saw black people getting were burial rights. His campaign was having a rally in a large downtown auditorium, and all the student groups who opposed his candidacy were planning to go and disrupt his party. George Wallace, a symbol of everything that was wrong in America, was bringing his hate-filled campaign to our town, and we were going to give him a taste of northern inhospitality.

We marched down the middle of Main Street to the auditorium and took seats in the middle so we could stand up and boo every time he tried to say something. Of course, Governor Wallace used that to his advantage.

In his southern drawl, he said, "You see, these communist loving radicals don't believe in freedom of speech. They believe in it for them, but not for you and me."

That made us get up and confirm what he had just said. We started booing and blowing whistles, but he kept on.

"I'll tell you what," he continued, pointing his finger in our direction. "If one of you dope smoking hippies gets in front of my car, I'll run you over, and I guarantee you won't be getting up to walk home."

The rest of his speech was a hate filled diatribe against everything but Aunt Jemima. The only things missing were the white sheets and a burning cross. A few fights broke out, and before the fun was over, we all got up and walked out singing *We Shall Overcome*, with our middle fingers in the air.

When we got outside the auditorium, the police started arresting people for disorderly conduct. They then forced us to walk away from the commercial shops toward a group of officers dressed in riot gear, waiting for an excuse to attack. From the back of our crowd a trio of guys hurled bags of shit at the police. Once the brown got all over their blue, it was payback time, and we were the checks being cashed. They fired tear gas into the crowd and made everyone scatter like bugs with the kitchen lights turned on. They arrested whoever they could catch, so I made a point to run faster than whoever was standing next to me. My heart was pounding, my eyes burning, my skin was on fire, and I had a hard time focusing, but eventually, I found a bus heading uptown and was able to escape the mayhem.

The first thing I did when I got home was to rip off my clothes and put them in a plastic bag. The hot water from the shower was soothing, but I still felt the burning effects of the tear gas.

That was my first taste of protest, and I ended up joining the Students for a Better Tomorrow to get involved in the movement. I spoke up at meetings and got to know the group's leaders. After one of our meetings, the group's chairman pulled me aside.

"Can I ask you something?" John Washington asked.

"Sure, what's up?"

"You've got some good ideas, and we're looking for guys like you to speak at meetings for us. Would you be interested in something like that?"

I was as excited as I was surprised and replied, "Sure. I wouldn't mind doing that."

John reached out and shook my hand. "That's great. You could help us out next week if you have some time."

"OK. Just let me know what you need."

After speaking at a few afternoon rallies, I became a featured speaker on campus. I also spoke to liberal groups off campus that wanted to understand what was happening with the student movement. Between that and the girls I was connecting with, the revolution business was working out OK for me.

During one of our meetings, we decided we didn't want any Defense projects on our campus. We also wanted ROTC to go the way of the fraternities that had been booted from campus a couple of years earlier. We bundled these issues with a few others and printed them up in a set of demands we presented to the University. We knew there was no way the school would ever approve those demands, but we made them anyway.

After the school refused to respond to our demands, the leadership team had another meeting. John Washington opened the meeting. "Hey everybody, we gave some reasonable demands to this school, and they completely ignored us. We have to let them know we're serious, so I want to give everybody a chance to voice their opinion on what we should do."

Laura Madison, our Communications Director, always looked for the most peaceful approach. "I think we should have a sit-in with non-stop prayer in front of the school until they agree to meet with us. Then, we can invite the local news media to cover it and put extra pressure on the school."

Bob Armstrong, our Director of Security, wanted to take a more confrontational approach.

"That won't work. What are you going to do if it rains?" Bob chuckled and continued. "Prayer only works in church."

"What do you think we should do?" I asked.

"I read about some students who took over a building and held the workers hostage. Then, they used that as leverage in their negotiations over their demands."

I looked at Bob and said, "That's a bit extreme. I think we should focus on one of our demands and take action related to that particular issue."

"That's a great idea," John said. "What do you think we should do?"

I stopped to think for a couple of seconds and replied. "I was thinking maybe we could destroy those two trailers they're using to do Defense research. We shouldn't be supporting the war machine on this campus."

Everyone except Laura agreed we would vandalize the two trailers leased by the Defense Department, on Sunday night when security would be at its lowest.

Eight people, organized by Bob Armstrong, walked over to the Project Themis trailer and jimmied the lock with a crowbar. We went inside, four men per trailer, and started throwing papers on the floor. We unplugged computers and pulled the ribbons out of the typewriters.

We finished vandalizing the two trailers before security could come and investigate. Even though we destroyed a lot of valuable property, the school thought we were misguided youths, and refrained from taking any punitive action. They thought they were being reasonable, but for us it was a green light for more action.

We finally got a meeting with the administration. It was attended by the Deans of the major university divisions and the head of the school's disciplinary committee, a man named Dick Cowsiggle. We called him the same thing we called the President, Tricky Dick, because like Nixon, he couldn't be trusted.

Dean Cowsiggle made the opening comments, "I first want to thank everybody for coming to this meeting. There's no better way to resolve differences than constructive dialogue."

John spoke for the group. "Thank you, Dean Cowsiggle. We wanted to take advantage of this opportunity to speak with you about the direction we'd like to see the university move in."

Dean Cowsiggle looked at our group and said, "I can't guarantee we're going to move in a direction you'd like, but I will hear you out, and if it makes sense, we'll see what we can do."

Don Spencer, a pre-law student who handled our legal affairs, asked, "When you say you'll see what you can do, exactly what does that mean? You can tell us that and then do nothing."

Dean Cowsiggle looked down at the floor, raised his head, and then replied, "I'm giving you my word. That's the best I can do."

Listening to a proven liar tell you to trust him is like asking a burglar not to break into your unlocked home. The odds are not good.

"OK," John said. "We can discuss four of our demands now and worry about the rest later." The idea was to not give them so much that it would take them years to implement.

"OK," one of the other Deans said. "I read about a dozen demands you kids want."

"We're not talking about all of them. We wanted to give you something easier to implement," I told the administration. "There should be no Defense research done here. We think ROTC should be moved off the campus, we think school should be a drug-arrest-free zone, and we want more diversity in the student population. These demands are not negotiable."

"First of all, everything's negotiable," said Dean Cowsiggle. "When you start a conversation saying you're not willing to compromise, you're not being very serious."

"We are serious," Bob said. "If you underestimate us, you'll find out the hard way."

"It's going to take us a few weeks to examine your demands and determine what it would take to implement them. Obviously, there are costs associated with some of these things, and we have to see whether our budgets can support them. So let's meet next month, and hopefully, I'll have some answers for you." With that, Dean Cowsiggle ended the meeting and walked us to the door.

We walked back to our office to debrief the meeting and plan our next steps.

"What did you guys think of that meeting?" John said to the group.

Don Spencer was the first to respond. "He gave us a bigger snow job than last winter. So when he says they have to look into it, that means nothing will get done."

"I agree," Bob said. "They're just looking to run out the clock. They want to put things off and hope things cool down over the summer. Tricky Dick didn't get that name for nothing."

"What do you think we should do?" I asked. "We need to have a Plan B. Just in case."

Don looked over at me and said, "I think we should wait until they respond. If we don't like the response, or get no response, then we will have to do something dramatic."

It made perfect sense to me. If it worked at other colleges, I didn't see why it couldn't work here. "If they don't meet our demands, we should take over the Administration Building. That'll bring them running back to the table."

"I agree," Bob said. "If we do the action at night, we won't have to worry about the administrative staff. They just won't be able to come to work the next day."

We took a vote on Don's strategy and Bob's plan and agreed to go move forward with the scheme if we didn't get the results we were looking for.

It had been three weeks since our meeting with The Administration. We hadn't heard any response from them and were nervous they were going to stall us for the rest of the school year. If that happened, it was going to be put up or shut up time for us.

Later that week we got a certified letter from Dean Cowsiggle thanking us for the meeting and responding to our wishes point by point. The letter said they couldn't eliminate Defense Department research because the government would sue the school for terminating the contract, and it would cost more money than the school could afford to lose. They couldn't set up a drug-free-arrest zone on campus because there were local, state, and federal jurisdictions involved, and any changes in the law had to come through the respective legislatures. They were looking into ROTC, but before they could move that function off campus, they had to find a new place for the program. He also said they believed in diversity and if we knew any qualified minorities, to send them to the admissions office. He thanked us again for bringing the issues to his attention, and he looked forward to discussing more mutual concerns in the future.

Everybody in the group was livid when they read the letter we had posted in our office. They knew the Administration had no intention of taking our demands seriously. For them, it was business as usual. In their minds they heard us, and now it was time to move on. But we weren't moving on. We were just getting started.

We held an impromptu rally at the back of the student union the next day. I took the bullhorn and started speaking. "Brothers and sisters, we've been talking to the Administration about getting our school out of the death business. We asked that all Defense research, much of which is used to kill our brothers and sisters in Viet Nam, be terminated. We asked that ROTC be removed from campus so we weren't training potential war criminals. We said we wanted more minority students admitted to this school, and that cops not be allowed to bust people on campus for the personal use of drugs. They agreed that admitting more minority students was a desirable goal, but they didn't have a plan to implement it. That means it's empty talk. They aren't going to do anything. We need to make them tell us why they can't implement a few changes."

"That's right brother, we need to go over there," a guy in the front row said.

"I don't know about you guys, but I'm going to walk over to the Administration Building to get some answers." I walked down the steps heading towards the Administration Building. "If anyone wants to join me, we can show them who really controls this university. It's us, and they need to know it."

The crowd shouted their approval. The crowd, which had started with about fifty people, and had grown to over four hundred, followed me to the Administration Building. They followed me and the SBT leadership. We forced our way into the building, allowing the office personnel to leave, and then we chain-locked the doors.

We had a meeting that evening with Dean Cowsiggle. "Before we can start negotiating anything," he said. "Agree to leave this building. Right now, you're trespassing, and we can't resolve anything while you're breaking the law."

John shouted back, "We're not leaving until you agree to our demands."

"We're still looking into some of this. I'm talking to law enforcement about your drug-arrest-free zone. The lawyers are looking over our Defense contracts, and if you know any qualified minorities, you can have them call our admissions office. I know this isn't what you wanted to hear, but these things take time."

"That's the same crock of crap you told us two months ago," Bob told him.

"It was true then, and it's still the truth today. These things take time. I've kept my word to you, and I'd like you to leave the building before anyone gets hurt. You all need to be gone by the time the staff gets here tomorrow morning. If you can do that, I promise we won't punish anyone for trespass."

After the college administrators left, we had a party with marijuana smoke so thick you could eat it with a fork. At one end of the hall, a group of people sat around a man and a woman playing guitars and singing protest songs. In the President's office, two people were having sex on his oriental carpet, and a makeshift bar serving wine and mixed drinks was set up in the Dean's office. I would bet that most people had forgotten why we had gone into the building. For many people, the party went on all night, but I found an empty office and crashed until the morning.

Rumors were spreading that the police were coming to forcefully take the building back. So I went out the back door with a couple of friends and rode by the local police precinct to either confirm or shoot down the rumors. Inside the front door you could see police dressed in riot gear and not planning on playing around with us. I might have been a revolutionary, but I wasn't letting the revolution get my ass kicked. I thought more than twice about not going back into the Administration building and waiting for the cops to get everybody else out. After all, I was already out, so why take the beating?

We drove back to school to let everyone know what we saw. We knew we were in no position to fight the police, so when they came and told us to leave in thirty minutes, we were gone in twenty-five. We retreated to the student lounge to talk about our great victory. We talked about our courageous stand against the police and how lucky they were for not beating us up and getting bad publicity.

After that near catastrophe, I quit the revolution and went back to being a student on the way to law school. I was surprised that summer when I got a letter stating that I was being expelled from school for engaging in riotous behavior, destroying school property, and breaking multiple school regulations. Tricky Dick had pulled another fast one. He had promised not to take punitive action for trespass, but the expulsion letter was from another department, for other offenses. Technically, he didn't take the action, but I was sure he gave his approval. The country was able to get rid of Tricky Dick Nixon, but Tricky Dick Cowsiggle was still at the university telling half-truths and full lies. The one good thing about being expelled from school was that I wouldn't have to hear either Tricky Dick again.

Part of the Problem

I had never been the center of a controversy before, but I was quickly becoming one of the most controversial people at my school. The major political organizations at school were threatening boycotts and disruptions, and I was the cause of it all. Letters were flowing into the school newspapers. Some praised me for *telling it like it was*, while others vilified me for being insensitive to the needs of my people.

The object of this furor was a play I starred in entitled *The Fare*. A two-man play set in a taxi, it featured a conservative white driver, while I played a seemingly more liberal black passenger.

"Where can I take you?" the driver asked.

"I'm going over to the Good Fortune Grill on Elmwood."

"I've never been in that place. I heard the food is real good."

"I'd have to agree with you on that," I replied.

"I was driving by there last week and they had a big demonstration out front. I think people protest too much in this country."

"How else can we get things to change?"

"Maybe things don't need to change so fast. I think you people are asking for a lot."

"We're only asking for rights we should already have. How long should we wait for that to happen?"

"I don't know. But you can't have everything at once."

"Which one of our rights do you think we should wait for? The protest you saw was for Open Housing."

"And I think that's wrong."

"You think people shouldn't be allowed to live in whatever community they can afford?"

"I don't think the government should tell me who I can sell my house to and who my neighbors should be."

"My friend, here's what you have to remember. The Declaration of Independence says all men are created equal and endowed with God given rights. Among those rights are the right to live, to be free, and to enjoy happiness. If I can't live where I can afford, then that's violating the founding document of this country."

"I never looked at it like that. I see your point. I didn't know many Negroes when I was growing up, but I guess you all can't be that bad."

I then pulled a gun from my coat and said, "We all aren't that bad, but I am. Now give me the money." I took the money, jumped out of the cab, and disappeared into the night.

When I tried out for the play, I had only read the script's first page. I hadn't acted in a while and was happy to be back on stage. When I finally read the entire script, I was as surprised at the ending as everyone else, but I justified it because I was only playing a fictional character. Open minded people in 1971 should have been able to handle that.

The writer/director of the play was a Theater major producing it as his final project. Michael Whitman claimed to have had friends in Hollywood, with standing offers for him to direct low budget films as soon as he graduated. He promised me I'd be the first person he called if he ever needed a black person in any of his movies. If I played my cards right, I could be the next Sidney Poitier. For that, all this was worth it.

Every Monday after class, I met friends in the student union. We would drink beer or coffee and argue about politics. The debates sometimes got very intense and often attracted large crowds, with strangers often jumping in and taking sides.

This Monday was no different than any other. I walked into the Rathskeller and saw my friend Bill sitting at a table with his girlfriend Anne and her friend Dolores. They were reading letters in the school newspaper about the play.

"Man, you're causing quite a stir with that play," Bill said.

"I don't know why people are so bent out of shape. All I'm doing is playing a role."

"People are saying you sold out," Bill continued.

"Sold out. I've got a part-time job, parking cars at a restaurant I can't afford to eat in."

Everyone was having fun talking about me and the play, and my friends were no different. Then, finally, Anne and Dolores started in.

"I hear we're the only sisters who will be seen with you," Dolores said.

"I'm surprised you guys aren't scared sitting here."

"We're telling people you're our uncle," Dolores teased.

Anne jumped in, "We just can't figure out which one, Tom or Remus." Everyone laughed.

Anne, who wore a short afro, and copper and African brass jewelry, explained her position. "The problem with the play is that it gives a false image of Black people to folks who have very little interaction with us. They need to see more positive images, and you aren't giving them one. The Black Panthers say either you're part of the solution or you're part of the problem, and right now, you're part of the problem."

"I don't know what's so hard to understand. I'm not portraying our race. I'm playing an individual."

"Amos n Andy" was about individuals, but it shaped how people perceived all of us. That's why people fought to get them off the air. It wasn't because they wanted to deprive the actors of work."

"She's right," Dolores said. "The only reason those people like this play is because your character reverts to their concept of how Black people act. The white guy grows in character while the brother goes from being semi-intelligent to a common criminal. That's why your boy wrote it that way. You need to work up a new ending."

I thought about what they were saying and knew in my heart they were right. "I'll have to talk to Mike about it."

I had initially enjoyed my celebrity status, but the longer the controversy went on, the more it started to bother me. I was tired of reading letters about myself in the school papers, tired of people's icy stares, and the deep freeze by the sisters.

I couldn't sleep more than four hours a night with nightmares at least three times a week. One night I dreamed during a performance of the play, a group of activists threw tear gas canisters into the gym and caused a stampede. People trampled anyone not fast or strong enough to make their way out the exit doors. The local police were called, and once everyone saw them, they started pelting them with bottles. The police began cracking heads with their clubs like they were taking batting practice. With people running in all directions, I was trying to find a safe way out. As I tried to escape, I was cornered by a mob accusing me of causing the ruckus, and they were going to make me pay. They closed in, threw a rope around a pipe in the ceiling, and tied the other end in a noose they placed around my neck. They made me stand on a chair to be kicked from under me. Before they could kick it out, I woke up, dripping with sweat, and my heart beating feverishly. That dream scared me so much I was still shaking two hours later.

I saw Michael later that week and told him my feelings.

"I've been getting a lot of heat about this play."

"So what! You're a celebrity."

"That's not the point. Have you heard about the proposed actions against us?"

"I don't pay attention to rumors?" he said.

"I do. Maybe we should rewrite the ending."

"Why would we want to do that? We need the controversy."

"But what about the socio-political implications?"

Michael turned to me and said, "Socio-political bullshit! You're an actor. Not a politician or a sociologist."

"That might be easy for you to say, but it's not so easy for me."

"When you're in the public eye, people are always going to be saying things. If they don't like what we're doing, they don't have to buy tickets."

"Can't we maintain the controversy with a better ending?"

"Have you forgotten why we moved the play from the Haas lounge to the gym? We've been sold out for over two months now."

"Yeah, but we're fostering stereotypes that have no place on a college campus."

"That's one of the reasons I want to move it off campus. No matter what we do, somebody's gonna be pissed off," Michael said. "All we can do is use it to our advantage."

"Have you heard the latest rumors on campus? I don't want to be responsible if somebody gets hurt."

"You're not responsible. If something breaks out, the campus police will have to deal with it."

"Yeah, but we can defuse some of this before it happens."

"Why would we change something that's working?"

Michael was totally insensitive to the feelings people were expressing on campus. As far as he was concerned, any disturbances would help him sell more tickets.

Everywhere I walked on campus I heard murmurs about actions being planned to shut down the play. Black and liberal white groups were contemplating a joint action, and people were scared there might be an effort to prevent people from entering the gym. One group threatened to print counterfeit tickets to fill the gym with their members and disrupt everything. There were even reports that tear gas canisters would be hurled into the gym. This sounded eerily similar to the nightmare I had earlier in the week. I didn't know if any of the rumors were true. For all I knew Michael might have been the source of the rumors, to increase ticket sales.

When I walked to the gym before the Friday performance, the pickets had already come to work, carrying placards and passing out leaflets. One conservative group, "The Young Free Americans" said they were prepared to physically challenge the pro-boycott groups. Another angry group lined up outside the gym to get good seats for the evening show. They didn't want anyone telling them they couldn't come to see the play.

I walked into the back entrance of the gym and saw Michael going over last-minute changes with the set designers.

"What's happening?" he asked.

"Did you see all those people outside?"

"It's great. I've been talking to some people about moving the play downtown because we're so hot everybody in town wants to see us."

"We're looking down the barrel of a potential blood bath, and all you're talking about is a bigger auditorium. There's an old proverb that says, either you're part of the solution or you're part of the problem, and right now we're big parts of a potential problem."

That evening the play went on as usual. I kept expecting someone to come rushing to the stage and lob a stink bomb onto the set. Worse yet, what if phony gunshots caused a stampede and people got crushed?

Throughout the first part of the performance I carried out the script as it was written. I robbed the cab driver as I was supposed to but signaled the technicians not to lower the curtain. Instead of letting the play end, I walked back to the cab driver and gave him back his money. I apologized and offered to buy him a drink. As we walked off the stage together, I signaled for the curtain to close. The crowd stood up and roared their approval giving us four curtain calls. The guy playing the cab driver was surprised at the new ending but went along with my improvisation. I saw Michael afterwards, and to my surprise, he shook my hand and said, "Great ending!" We used the new ending in our subsequent performances, and it defused the controversy. I felt good knowing I was no longer part of a problem.

Better Living Through Chemistry

During the Reagan Presidency, the United States was fighting a losing battle in the war on drugs. Crack was creeping into suburban schoolyards, heroin was making a comeback, and cocaine was being used openly in some of the most famous clubs in the country. Nancy Reagan often spoke to children too young for this to be a serious problem, and never reached out to the people who really needed her help. Based upon the information in her unauthorized biography, Nancy and Ronnie, at one time in their lives had a hard time saying no like the rest of us. I could never understand why it was OK for her and Ronnie to toke up, while the rest of us were condemned to a life with the Marlboro man.

Hallucinogenic drugs had been used as a part of religious ceremonies by native people for thousands of years before there were happy hippies flying around in imaginary aircraft.

Different decades spawned different types of drug usage. Cab Calloway sang about the reefer man in the 1930's. During the 40's and 50's, heroin was used to cheat jazz musicians out of their wages, and during the 1960's, LSD and marijuana became the drugs of choice for the new counterculture. Drug use became a uniting badge that tied many young people together against the dominant culture that controlled our cultural mores.

Acid, the commonly used name for LSD, was generally taken with friends. There was always one person not tripping in case there was a need to talk someone down from a bad trip, or get them to a hospital.

I remember the first time I took acid. It was my sophomore year in college, and I was hanging out at a concert being held to welcome returning students. The group playing was called Alice Cooper, though there were no women in the group. What they played had a hard time passing for music. The only good thing about this concert was that it was free and even then, it wasn't worth the money. They sprayed fire extinguishers at the crowd and threw chicken feathers around the stage. During their final song, they decapitated some dolls they kept in a wooden box on the stage. Just when we thought it couldn't get weirder, they finished the set by smashing their equipment. They did everything but play good music.

Against this backdrop I would experience what I intellectually understood and always wanted to do, but never quite put the pill in my mouth.

During the intermission I walked out of the venue and ran into a friend I had met the year before. Kevin was a Timothy Leary devotee with long brown hair tied back in a ponytail. He wore a cowboy shirt and brown Frye boots.

"Hey man, how was your summer?" he asked.

"It was good. What about yours?"

"I went out to Arizona and stayed with friends, and it was great. We dropped acid and sat in the desert watching the natural order of the universe."

"Sounds like some pretty heavy stuff."

"Yeah man. The most intense experience I ever had."

"I always wanted to try it but got scared of having a bad trip."

"There's no such thing as a bad trip. That was invented by the media to scare people from using acid. Trips are what you make them. If you fill your head with negative thoughts, then your journey will be challenging. But, if you concentrate on peace and love, you'll have a beautiful trip every time."

"I'll remember that when I finally try it."

"Do you want a hit?" he asked. "I have some great stuff I brought back from Arizona?"

"That sounds really cool, but I'm not carrying any money."

"Don't worry about it. It's my treat." Kevin handed me a little orange pill that I put in my shirt pocket.

I took the acid before the band got back on stage, hoping it would make the music sound better, but the second half was worse than the first.

I kept waiting for the acid to kick in, but it never did. Finally, I figured it was as bad as the music, so I gave up on both and caught the next bus back to my apartment to prepare for a German test.

I got home and opened my German textbook, reading the material to be covered in the test. My roommate Mike was frying some chicken for a late dinner when my jeans turned from a faded blue to multi-colored swirls of paisley. The chicken on my plate started speaking, suggesting I become a vegetarian, and the acid I had taken four hours earlier, was beginning to take me on a ride.

I turned to my roommate and said, "I don't want to trip now. I've got a German test in the morning and an anti-war speech in the afternoon."

If everything I had read about acid was right, it would be hours before I came down. So my roommate and I decided to visit some friends who could give us a couple of joints.

We went to the apartment of some girls we knew who always had good pot, and I figured I'd smoke my way down from the trip. This was a dumb strategy that had no chance of succeeding. After I smoked the joint, my hallucinations increased, and I was higher than ever. My mind raced in a thousand directions at the same time, with no sense of linear time or space. We were walking back to our apartment when my roommate suddenly appeared thirty feet ahead of me.

I yelled out, "Hey Mike, wait for me."

He looked at me, shook my arm, and asked, "Are you alright?"

I turned to him and said, "Holy shit, what the hell was that?"

We continued walking towards his car when the same thing happened again. He appeared to be walking a block and a half ahead this time, and again grabbed my arm, "Are you sure you're OK?".

"Yeah," I replied, but I wasn't really sure.

Mike suggested we drive across town and pick up my girlfriend, who had done a lot of reading about acid, but also never took any. But she could intellectually tell you everything you wanted to know about tripping, so we got into his Volkswagen and headed across town.

The ride across town seemed like I was traveling through the galaxies in a four-wheeled spaceship. Fifteen minutes later, a blue and white police car started following us. In my condition, this was the last thing I needed. What would happen if they pulled us over? What if they decided to engage in a little police brutality? A lot of bad things could happen, and my brain wasn't prepared to handle any of them. Another terrifying thought flashed across my mind. What if this scene wasn't real? What if it was just another hallucination? I could be freaking out for nothing. I tried to slow down my thinking when I saw the police car's red and blue lights blinking. The car pulled up on the side and told Mike to pull over. I had to be cool because spending time in jail and tripping on acid were not complementary activities.

The biggest policeman I had ever seen walked up to Mike's window and asked him to roll it down. I sat still and tried not to look at the officer. As hard as I tried not to look, my peripheral vision kept glancing in his direction. His head started expanding. First, it was normal, then it turned into a Mr. Potato Head with a toothpick for a nose and two jellybeans for eyes. He knocked on the window and created a noise so loud my hearing started to fade. Then his head went from looking like an Idaho potato to looking like a Halloween pumpkin. The hand he used to knock on the window started generating extra fingers. Initially, he had a normal five, until I saw seven fingers on his right hand. While all this was going on, I kept quiet and tried not to freak out.

The officer's voice sounded like it was coming from the back of a cave. Everything he said was echoing, with the duplicate phrase being louder than the original.

"How are you guys doing tonight?" He looked around the car and then said to Mike, "Can I have your license and registration?"

Mike took them out of his wallet to hand to the officer, who reached into the car with an arm that moved faster than a lizard's tongue, and snatched the papers out of Mike's right hand. He looked at them for what seemed like thirty-five minutes before walking back to his car and calling in Mike's information to see if he was wanted for anything. It seemed as if days had passed before he got out of his car and walked back to us. "Can I ask where you boys are going?" As he spoke, the officer started growing taller with each word. By the time he finished speaking, he had gone from being average height to over seven feet tall, and the taller he got, the squeakier his voice became. I wanted to laugh but was too scared to crack a smile.

Mike replied, "We're going over to State College to pick up a friend."

"Alright. You can go," he told us. "Just make sure you boys don't get into any trouble." He handed Mike his papers with the same lizard-like motion he used to take them, and we continued our trek to pick up my girlfriend, who was going to sit with me through the remainder of my acid trip.

My girlfriend Susan was waiting in the lobby of her dorm when we pulled up in Mike's car. When she saw the car, she came out and got in the back seat. Though it wasn't Halloween, Susan was dressed like the wicked witch in *The Wizard of Oz.* She even had a walking stick that doubled as a flying broom.

During the entire ride back to my apartment, she only spoke to Mike. It was as if I wasn't there. Her voice sounded like a ten-year-old, with a very high undeveloped pitch. When we got back to my place, Susan gave me a kiss that swallowed half of my face. I looked in the mirror and saw a dark shade of lipstick covering my mouth and a good part of my cheek. I tried to rub it off, but when I wiped my mouth, no lipstick ever got on the tissue.

While I sat in the middle of the floor listening to Crosby Stills and Nash, Susan ate the rest of the chicken Mike had made and poured herself a glass of wine to drink with her meal.

One of my roommates came running down the stairs dressed in a poorly fitted bathrobe and shouted, "What's going on down here? I'm trying to get some sleep." Jeff was the oddball roommate we never asked for. He liked to box in his spare time, and possessed anger management issues that didn't go well with his hobby. He always sounded like he wanted to punch something.

Mike looked at Jeff and said, "Richie's taking a little trip, so I went and got his girlfriend to sit with him until he comes down."

Jeff replied, with uncharacteristic empathy, "OK. Just keep the music down." He then went back upstairs to his bedroom and drifted back to sleep.

Susan and I tried having sex, but I couldn't focus long enough to keep things going. I was up and down like a roller coaster and was sure that was no fun for her. I was about as reliable as a broken car engine.

I didn't sleep that night and still hadn't figured out what to do about the German test. I didn't want to fail, so I figured I'd skip class, find out what was on the test from my friends, and then take a makeup later.

I think I became a better person after having taken my trip. I gained new insights into the human brain I could have never gained any other way. The Dow Chemical Company had a slogan that many kids in my generation took to heart. Dow believed that America would succeed by *Better Living with Chemistry.* We believed that too. We just were using different chemicals.

The Birthday Party

My college roommate Morris and I were born during the same month, of the same year, at opposite ends of the same day. We were similar in many respects but presented two different personalities at other times. Morris was a kind, gullible soul, while I usually thought about how a situation was going to benefit me. It wasn't that I didn't care about other people's thoughts or feelings, I was just more concerned with my own. This was the reason my last girlfriend ended our relationship. She would call me selfish, but I would always explain in great length that I wasn't selfish, only self-oriented, which was a different type of egocentricity. I remember our last fight.

"You are the most egotistical person I have ever met," she said.

"I'm not egotistical," I replied. "I just like what I like and see no reason to accept less."

"So, you're saying your way is the only way? And nobody else's opinions matter."

"No, I'm saying my opinion matters more to me."

"And what about my opinion? How much does that matter to you?"

"It matters, but I'm not going to tell you it matters more than mine, because it doesn't, and I mean that with all due respect."

"I'm looking for a man to be my equal, not my superior, and I don't think this is going to work out."

That was the last time I heard from or saw Morgana.

It was the beginning of the fall semester, Morris and I had a birthday approaching, and we talked about doing something special. We were going to be twenty and wanted to do something different. When we thought about what we could afford, it was clear this was not going to be a money-is-no-object birthday. The more we discussed what we wanted to do, the more we realized what we couldn't. We couldn't afford to fly to Florida, and I didn't want to go to Boston, so that wasn't leaving much for two east-coast college kids in search of a significant twentieth birthday experience. We called friends at different schools but couldn't come up with any place worth visiting.

Morris got a call from a friend attending school in Binghamton. He said the Grateful Dead was going to be playing at his school, and he could get us tickets for the concert, plus a place to crash for the weekend. With no better options, it looked like our significant experience would take place in a small town where some of the families still lived on farms.

"Hey, Morris, what are we supposed to do in such a small town?"

"That's the beauty of it. The chicks have nowhere to go. I heard even the ugly guys get laid there. "

In 1970 one of our favorite modes of transportation was hitchhiking. In those days you didn't have serial killers and other miscellaneous miscreants driving up and down the highways. It wasn't uncommon to see young people with knapsacks on roads and highways all over the country. All it took to get anywhere was a protruding thumb on the end of an outstretched arm.

Once the word got out about the concert, there was a psychedelic armada traveling down the New York Thruway to Binghamton. Volkswagens were packed with as many as six people riding down the highway to see the gurus of acid rock. With all these folks driving to Binghamton, we had no trouble getting a ride.

When we arrived at Harpur College we called Morris' friend Howard Gold. They grew up together in Oceanside, and Morris often referred to him as his other brother. After meeting Howie, I could see why. They were about the same height, had curly brown hair in what we called a Jewish Afro, and thick mustaches covering their upper lips. They had similar facial structures, but Howie had blue eyes, and Morris' were brown. The sound of their voices was so similar I could close my eyes and not know which one was speaking.

Howie got the tickets for the concert but had less success getting us a place to sleep. His roommate had visitors who were supposed to have left, but when they heard the "Dead" were going to be there, they decided to stay another week. Three people were already sleeping on the floor, and the only way we could have slept there was if we slept in shifts. Howie said he was sure something would come through.

We spent the afternoon in Howie's room, listening to music and getting stoned.

"Hey Howie," I said. "Thanks for getting us these tickets. I think the show is going to be great."

"It's gonna be wild. I'm really sorry about the room though. I didn't know those guys were staying this weekend."

"Don't worry about it. I'm sure we'll find a place to crash," I assured him.

Howie got up, walked over to a little refrigerator on the other side of the room, and took out a plate of brownies which he put on his desk. Then, he went back to the fridge, took out a bottle of wine, and came back with the bottle and three glasses.

"Happy birthday guys." Howie lit a joint and passed it to Morris, who took two hits and passed it to me.

"You guys have to try these brownies. I made them especially for you." Howie laughed, picked up a knife, and cut the brownie into six equal pieces.

"What kind of brownies are these?" Morris asked.

"They're made Moroccan hash. We are going to be so wasted. The Grateful Dead would expect no less from us," Howie replied. We picked up our cups, held them in the air, and said cheers.

"So, Howie," Morris said. "What about the women? I heard even ugly guys get laid here."

"That's right. But I'm not sure that'll help you."

"What's wrong with me? I'm good-looking!" Morris exclaimed.

"You have to have a little bit of a game, and the last time I checked, yours was pretty weak."

"You've been saying that ever since I stole your girlfriend in high school."

"You didn't steal her. I gave her to you."

"You still didn't answer my question. How can we meet some girls?"

"We can go to the concert early, and it should be easy for both of you guys to connect."

An hour after eating those brownies, we almost forgot where we were and stared for what seemed like hours, at the psychedelic posters on the wall. We were feeling pretty good. All we had to do now was meet some girls and we'd be set. Anyone looking into Howie's room would have seen what resembled a Shanghai opium den. Howie's room wasn't the only drug den on the floor either. The pungent smell of dope was so strong, you could get high standing in the hall. We finally summoned enough strength to go to the gym to get a good place to stand for the concert.

We got to the gym two hours before the show, and it was already three-quarters full. *Sympathy for the Devil* was playing on the sound system, and we could close our eyes and visualize Mick Jagger standing there, wearing his American flag shirt, gyrating his hips with his shoulder length hair flying in his face. People negotiated small drug purchases in the row behind us.

An "acid rescue station" was set up In the back of the gym to help people having bad trips. Although the concert hadn't started, there were already three people having a rough time. One guy thought he was Napoleon and pleaded to be returned to Elba. One woman claimed to have seen the history of the world and could tell us our fates. Another woman thought she was dying and wanted suggestions as to what she should come back as. She was sure she would be reincarnated as a hen but wanted to come back as a swan gliding across a pond in an unspoiled aquatic habitat. They were all in bad shape and were being treated with vitamin C, and bottomless glasses of orange juice. While these three struggled to hold onto their last strands of sanity, everyone else was trying to give theirs up. Joints were being passed around and orange juice spiked with LSD traveled from row to row. With the exception of having nowhere to sleep, this was one of the best birthday parties I had ever had.

The lights in the gym were turned down, a hush came over the crowd, and six musicians came from behind the stage, taking their places on the bandstand. They dressed like the people in the audience, with long hair, tie-dyed clothes, and all the other regalia of the 60's counterculture. Finally, the lights were turned back up, and the "Dead" came to life.

"Hey man," I said to Morris. "Whatever you do, don't drink the orange juice with the black tape on the bottom."

"Why?" he asked. "Is there something wrong with it?"

"Yeah. It's spiked with acid."

"I did drink some juice, but I didn't look at the bottom. It tasted like orange juice."

I caught the attention of this girl standing in the row behind me. I would look at her and smile and then turn around. I noticed, out of the corner of my eye, that she was also checking me out. She was wearing a lavender tie-dyed T-shirt and black jeans with brown Fred Braun shoes. She had black hair and brown eyes and could have been on the cover of Ebony magazine. After checking her out for over an hour, I made my move.

"Would you like a hit?" I asked, and offered her the joint I was smoking

"Thanks!" she took a few puffs and gave it back.

"Do you go to school here, or are you visiting too?"

"I'm a junior here!" she replied.

"My roommate and I came down from Buffalo to celebrate our birthday."

"Happy Birthday! How has it been so far?"

"It's getting better as we speak. My name's Richie." I reached out and gave her hand a light shake.

"I'm Leola," she replied.

"Pleased to meet you," I looked around the gym and noticed we were the only black people there.

"So, where are you from?"

"St. Albans Queens," she replied. "What about you?"

"Born and raised in the Bronx," I replied. "So, what's your major?"

"English lit. What about you?"

"Right now, It's Political Science, but that could change."

"Are you staying with your friend tonight?"

"Not really. His roommate has some guys crashing who were supposed to be leaving but changed their minds after they heard about the concert."

"My roommate is away for the weekend, and if you want, you can stay in her bed."

That was all I needed to hear. After that, I was ready to skip the rest of the concert. It had been going on for over four hours and we were both tired.

"You don't have to leave if you don't want to," she said.

"I've seen the Dead several times, so I'd rather hang out with you. I just need to tell my roommate I'm leaving."

I went to speak to Morris but didn't see him or his buddy, Howie, anywhere. By the time I found Morris, his mind was traversing another galaxy.

"Rich, I can't find my hands! Do you remember where I left them? I can't find them!"

"Did you drink from the containers with the tape on the bottom?"

"I thought those were the ones you said were alright."

"No, those were the ones that were spiked!"

"I've been drinking from them all night. Rich, why is that grizzly bear playing guitar on stage?"

"I better take you to the rescue station."

"Why did you call me Morris? That's not my name! I'm Captain Nemo!"

I had some very difficult choices to make. I didn't want to leave Morris at the concert by himself, and I wasn't bringing him with me to Leola's. The best place I could think of was the rescue center. He'd have a place to stay when he came down off the trip, and they'd feed him breakfast in the morning. This sounded like a pretty good deal to me, and I could still spend the night with Leola.

By now, Morris was babbling incoherently about life after death in the Middle Ages. This only helped confirm my decision to dump him in the rescue center.

When we got to the rescue center, it looked like Bellevue on Christmas eve. Most of the people being checked in were physically there, but nowhere to be found mentally. The three people I had seen initially were still there. Other people were crying hysterically or sitting in the middle of the floor, laughing like hyenas. One guy said he was Richard Nixon preparing to give a press conference. Only three counselors were in the center, trying to deal with over thirty people. Somehow, I didn't think Morris would get the right attention and decided this wasn't the best place to leave him. I'd have to sit up with him for the rest of the evening, and as much as I hated it, I had to tell Leola that I wasn't coming back to the dorm with her. Morris and I had come down together to celebrate our birthday, and I wasn't going to leave him with a bunch of freaked-out acid heads. I told Leola I'd call her before I went back to Buffalo. Morris and I left the gym, went back to Howie's dorm, and headed down to the basement. We found an unoccupied corner and sacked out on two green sofas. While I was at the rescue center, I picked up a small bottle of vitamin C and a half gallon of non-spiked orange juice to give Morris. This would help ease him off his trip. I fed him the vitamins, gave him several glasses of the orange juice, and listened to him create unbelievable stories until he drifted off to sleep.

Peace Love and
My Best Friend's Sister

I was shocked when I heard the voice on the other end of the phone. It had been nearly fifteen years since we had spoken. What had once been a strong relationship disintegrated like a sandcastle washed away by a 20-foot wave hitting the shore. Two peas that had once occupied the same pod were now packed in separate cans, and neither of us could have ever imagined this happening. But it did. We were victims of the times we grew up in. Victims of the pervasive ignorance and bigotry we inherited from previous generations. We thought we were a generation that would change things, and for a while, we did. But like all things swimming against the tide, our good intentions became swallowed up by the culture of intolerance that preceded us.

George and I became friends the first day I attended our city's most exclusive boy's school. I knew my athletic ability was the only reason I was given a scholarship. I was brought in to help win championships, and for my participation in football, basketball, and track, my family wouldn't have to pay the twelve thousand dollar annual tuition. I also got free lunch every day. In 1968, that was more than the pay of a significant portion of the adult population. Harvard didn't cost that much, but this high school for the sons of privilege did. Without my ability to run fast and jump high, my shadow would have never darkened their doorway. George and I connected on the first day of football practice.

"Hey man," he said to me. "Did anybody tell you this was practice? That was a pretty hard lick you put on me."

"My dad always says you play like you practice, so for me, practice is no different than the game."

"I'm glad you're on our side," he laughed. "My name's George Cooper," he said while extending his hand. "But everybody calls me Coop." Coop was tall, with short dirty blond hair, and sideburns that ended at the bottom of his earlobes. He had an oval face that most women would find attractive.

"My name's Spencer." I shook his hand, glad to have seemingly made a friend.

From then on, Coop and I were inseparable. We ate lunch together, went to the movies together, and even snuck into bars with our phony ID cards. Usually, when you saw one of us, the other wasn't too far behind. That all ended after we graduated. That's when our roads started following different paths. Coop's family got him into Princeton, while I won a scholarship to the local State University. We kept in touch, but the friendship we once had was changing.

The summer after our freshman year in college, Coop heard about a music festival being held in the Catskills. He asked me if I wanted to meet him, his cousin Jim, and his sister, Sandy. The festival featured Jimi Hendrix, Richie Havens, The Jefferson Airplane, and just about every major rock group except the Rolling Stones and the Beatles. For only twenty-four dollars, this could be a weekend I wouldn't forget.

I remember meeting Sandy the first time Coop invited me over for dinner. We were watching the news when she sat down in a chair in the middle of the room. She looked like a female version of Coop, with the same color hair and the same oval face. Even though he was a year older than she, they could have passed for twins.

"Anything interesting in the news?" she asked.

"There was a pretty big demonstration in Washington this afternoon. The police went crazy on the demonstrators," Coop replied.

"It serves them right," Sandy said.

"I don't think it serves anyone right to have the police beat up innocent students," I told her.

Sandy looked at me and retorted. "They should have thought about that before they decided to shut down traffic in the nation's capital."

"Some things are a little more important than a traffic jam," Coop told her.

"You wouldn't say that if you were in an ambulance and couldn't get to a hospital."

"Does that mean we shouldn't voice our opinions if we don't like what our government is doing?" I looked at her and continued. "That's why we have the first amendment."

Sandy pointed her finger and replied, "If those people don't like what the government is doing, they can always go live somewhere else."

"What about fixing the things we don't like," Coop chipped in. "We can't get better if we don't own up to our shortcomings."

"This is the greatest country in the world. We don't have shortcomings."

I jumped back into the discussion. "When we allow people to live wherever they can afford, we eliminate job discrimination, and we provide equal education for everyone, we'll be even greater."

"I guess everybody's got a right to be wrong, and you're well within your rights." She laughed, got up, and left the room.

Coop and I laughed at her arguments, which mirrored the views of the Young Americans for Freedom, a right-wing student organization that didn't believe in universal freedom. They didn't support civil rights, or women's rights, and felt social change should come at glacier speed. They thought our effort in Vietnam was honorable and kept the United States from becoming the next Soviet Union. Sandy was neither a racist nor what we called a fascist pig. She was a William Buckley-style conservative who intellectually argued her small-government beliefs.

***

I was spending the summer with my aunt, who lived outside of New York City, and read about the rock festival Coop had talked about. For the opportunity to see current and future rock legends, the twenty-four dollar weekend admission was a steal. One of my co-workers and I bought tickets and agreed to drive his car to the concert.

The sun was shining with no hint of precipitation when we left Peekskill that morning. It started as a peaceful drive to the venue before we ran into a traffic jam bigger than the Washington D.C beltway. We went from driving five miles an hour above the speed limit to watching people walk five miles an hour faster than our car, and there were thousands of them. As far as your eyes could see, the people kept coming. Walking with their belongings slung across their backs, they marched towards what they thought would be a musical nirvana. Vans, trucks, and cars stuffed with more people than legally allowed, flooded the highways. Radio reports kept repeating the message that the roads leading to the concert were closed. We were concerned about the possibility of not getting in and having to turn around and go home. We ended up leaving the car on the side of the road and started walking the rest of the way. Fifteen minutes later, some people gave us a ride on the hood of their car for the final three miles. We had no idea this many people were showing up and were ill-prepared to deal with the consequences. We had no tents or food and had figured if we got hungry, we'd just leave the concert and find a nearby restaurant. This made as much sense as adding two and two and coming up with seventeen.

When we finally arrived at the festival site, which was not in the town of Woodstock, I didn't see where they were taking the tickets. By this time, the fences had been torn down, and the venue declared a free concert. Half a million people were hanging out on this farm, getting stoned, bathing in the sun, and soaking up the positive energy. Coop was better prepared for the weekend than I was. He had brought the family trailer with tents and a fully stocked refrigerator. The original plan was to meet in the front row center stage, but with this huge crowd, that was impossible.

Shortly after arriving, I heard a familiar voice calling my name. "Hey Spencer, don't go anywhere or we'll never find you again." It was Sandy carrying a small bottle of water.

I gave her a hug and introduced her to my friend. "This is Arnold. We drove up here together."

She shook Arnold's hand and told us to follow her back to their campsite. They had an extra tent they gave us to set up. After we set up the tent, we all sat in a circle and passed around a pipe filled with Lebanese hash.

"Hey Sandy," I said. "This doesn't look like your wine and cheese crowd." I laughed and passed her the pipe.

"How about declaring a truce for this weekend, she suggested. "No politics. Just some fun in the sun."

"I'm with you on that." We shook hands even though she didn't know how to do the current power handshake, so I tried to teach her. "If we're going to declare a truce, you have to at least know how to do the right handshake."

"What do you want from me? I'm a white girl who voted for Richard Nixon."

We all laughed and headed to the hill to find a good place to listen to the music. We were at least half a mile away from the stage, but the sound system was so good we rocked and rolled to every beat as if we were sitting in front of the stage. Everywhere you looked people were drinking wine, smoking joints, with some brave souls tripping out on acid. There were more people at this concert than lived in all but one city in New York state, and we had no idea how we were going to take care of some of the real necessities of life, like showering and going to the bathroom.

We split into two groups to find the answers. Sandy and I went to find showering possibilities while Coop and Arnie went to look for bathrooms. Sandy and I painstakingly walked through the crowd stepping over and around endless groups of people. Our plan was to find a cheap motel room we could rent for the weekend and take turns using the facilities. We never found that motel, but we did find a little pond tucked away in a corner of the farm that no one seemed to have discovered.

"Wow. Look at this cute little pond," Sandy said. "Let's go for a swim."

"First of all, I don't have my trunks, and second, we don't have any towels."

"Oh Spencer," she said. "You sound so lame. Who needs a bathing suit? There's no one here, and we can dry off in the sun."

Sandy and I had been friends for nearly five years, and the most I had ever seen of her was in a bikini. But now she was going to bare it all.

"I'm going in," she said. She pulled her tie-dyed t-shirt over her head and flung it to the ground. She turned her bra around, unhooked it, and threw it on the ground next to her shirt. She then slipped out of her shorts, pulled off her panties, and jumped headfirst into the water. "The water's fine. Why don't you come in?"

I got a rise out of seeing her naked body in the water and had a hard time keeping my democratic principles in check. I was wondering what Coop would have thought about this. A friend's sister was generally out of bounds without your friend's permission.

"Do I have to pull you in?" she joked. "You're not scared of the water, are you?"

I took off my clothes and jumped into what I hoped would be a cold shower. Instead of cooling me down, the warm water drove us together in a passionate embrace. We intimately kissed each other for the first time, and it felt like the best kiss I had ever experienced. Without saying anything, we waded out of the pool and laid down under the big sycamore tree where we had tossed our clothes, and for the first time, enjoyed each other's sexual proclivities. Ninety minutes later we were walking back to the tents. I couldn't believe I had just had sex with Sandy. I wondered what Coop would have thought about it, but I wasn't going to tell him. If Sandy wanted him to know, then that was her prerogative.

Later that night while everyone was sleeping, I crawled into Sandy's tent, and we continued where we had left off at the pond. We spent the rest of the weekend enjoying more sex, drugs, and rock and roll, with no one knowing anything about the sex part of it. When Monday came, we packed up the gear and headed to our respective destinations. Sandy, Coop, and Jim drove back to western New York while Arnie and I headed back to the New York City suburbs.

Sandy went to Smith College in Boston, and I was surprised to not hear from her for a couple of months. When she finally did call, she said she was going to be in town that next weekend and wanted to see me. We agreed to meet at a restaurant we all used to drink in. After sharing all the usual pleasantries, she looked me in the face and said, "I have to tell you something."

"What's going on?" I asked.

"I'm pregnant."

"Who's the father?"

"You're the only person I've been within the last six months," she replied.

Abortions were not legal at that time, so we didn't have a lot of choices. Marriage was an option I wasn't quite ready for, but I was sure she didn't want to have a black baby by herself.

"Have you told anyone in your family?"

"I just found this out last week. My parents would hit the roof if they knew about this, and I would be cut out of their will. They're OK with you and Coop being friends, but they would never want a black son-in-law or grandchild."

I was having a hard time coming up with the right words to say. "I'll support any decision you make. Just let me know what you want to do."

"I have a friend who knows a doctor who might be able to help."

"Is there anything I can do?"

"I don't think so," she replied. "I can't afford to quit school. Me and the baby would become the black sheep of our family, and that wouldn't be fair to me or the baby."

I understood her point. That next day she confided in her brother, and he called me madder than Dante's seventh ring of hell.

"Spencer," he said. "I thought you and I were friends."

"We are friends," I replied.

"Then why did I find out from my sister that the two of you were sneaking around behind my back."

"We didn't mean for it to happen."

"Things like that just don't happen. She didn't get pregnant by herself."

That was the last time I had heard from or spoken with him until that phone call, and there was nothing I could say. I had broken one of the unwritten rules of friendship and had no idea Sandy would become pregnant. I assumed she was taking birth control but should have confirmed that before I pulled my pants off.

"For what it's worth, I really loved your sister. Maybe it was a case of opposites being attracted. If it were a different time, maybe we could have made different decisions, but it wasn't a different time, and she decided what she thought was in her best interest, and I went along with it."

"The time had nothing to do with you telling me what was going on. I wouldn't have objected because you were my best friend."

"Coop, I was wrong and should have told you when it happened. I know it's too late for apologies, but I am sorry, and I hope at some point we can become friends again. Your sister determined how everything played out. I even offered to marry her, but she didn't want that. I miss her friendship and yours as well."

"She'd be happy to know that," he said.

"How is she? Hopefully, she's OK."

"No Spence, she's not. She passed away last week, and I just thought you should know."

"Oh my God, I'm so sorry to hear that. Is there anything I can do?"

"No, we're OK," he replied.

He hung up the phone while I sat there, unable to move. I thought about our debates and the dancing and drinking we did. Even though those things would never happen again, I'll never forget that weekend of peace, love, and sex with my best friend's sister.

White Girls

Sly and the Family Stone was playing at the Inferno that evening. All week I had been looking forward to seeing them for the first time since Woodstock. This was a new type of black music. Following the likes of Jimi Hendrix and the Chambers Brothers, Sly and his group didn't wear slick sharkskin suits or have the choreographed dance moves of the Temptations. They jumped up and down to the rhythm and energy of their music. Wearing suede fringe jackets and sporting big afros instead of the processed hair worn by many of the black entertainers in the 60's, they were everyday people getting ready to dance to the music in a place where everybody could be a star.

"Hey man, you ready to go?" my brother asked. "The girls are waiting for us."

"I just gotta finish rolling another joint for the ride. We can't see Sly without letting him take us higher."

I finished rolling the joint and put it in my gold-plated cigarette holder. We were still waiting for my friend Tom, who was going to ride out with us. We were then going to go to my brother's school to pick up some lady friends who were going to smoke some dope with us and check out the music.

My brother had just transferred to this girl's school that had just started allowing men to attend. This was a young man's dream. This deal was so good I had him cut me in on the action, and I got more than my share of phone numbers.

Tom finally arrived, we jumped in my brother's car, and headed across town to pick up the girls. I sorted through the eight-track tapes in the glove compartment and found the latest album from the Chambers Brothers. We were singing *The Time has Come Today* as we pulled onto the girl's campus. They jumped in the car happy to see us. One of the girls twisted the cap off a bottle of wine and poured a cup for everyone. We were already stoned but I lit up a joint for the girls. From where I sat, life could not be better. Beautiful women, good music, and wacky weed. Who could want more than that? We finished the joint and headed for the Inferno.

Fifteen minutes after we had picked up the girls, a police car passed us, and apart from our normal dope induced paranoia, we paid them no mind. Five minutes later, another police car appeared in the rear-view mirror, but this time the lights were flashing and the siren blaring. He pulled us over, got out of his car, and walked up to my brothers' window.

"Can I ask where you boys are going?" He glanced at the girls but kept focusing on the men.

My brother replied, "We're going to The Inferno."

"Is that right?" the officer asked the girls sitting in the back. "Where do you know these boys from?"

"We go to school together," MaryBeth told him.

"Is that all you do?" the officer continued.

"I don't know what you're trying to say but we're just friends out to dance and listen to some music. That's it." MaryBeth sat back and regained her composure.

The officer turned to my brother and said, "OK, friend, let me see your license and registration."

My brother took his wallet from his back pocket and handed his license and registration to the officer, who took them and walked back to his car. It was a good thing we had disposed of the wine bottle, or I was sure we would have been cited for public intoxication.

The officer returned, pointed his flashlight at the inspection sticker on the front windshield, and noticed it had expired five days earlier.

"Driver. I need you to get out of the car and put your hands on the hood."

My brother got out of the car and did exactly what the officer told him. "Is there a problem officer?"

"You're driving with an expired inspection sticker. That's against the law."

"I've been taking exams in school all week and didn't realize it had expired."

"That's not a good excuse. It's your responsibility to know when your car needs to be inspected. We wouldn't want you driving an unsafe vehicle on our roads."

"You're right," my brother said. We were all hoping he would give us a ticket and let us go, but we weren't that lucky.

The policeman told my brother, "I need you to put your hands behind your back." When my brother put his hands behind his back, the officer placed him in handcuffs and put him in the squad car. He then told us to get out of the car. We were stranded in this small town with no taxis or buses and told we needed to go back to wherever we came from. They called a tow truck and impounded my brother's car.

I looked at one of the officers and asked, "How are we supposed to get back?"

The officer grinned and said, "Well, that's your problem, isn't it?"

I ended up calling a cab from the next town over and went home after dropping the girls at their dorm. What was going to be a night of sex, drugs, and rock and roll, turned out to be a night of jail, bail, and unfulfilled desires. The next day I went back to the scene of the crime to get my brother out of jail. I posted the fifty-dollar bail to get him released, and we received an evening court date three weeks away.

Since I forked out the fifty bucks to get my brother released, we didn't have any money left for a lawyer. The town we were in didn't have legal aid, so we cashed in our only chips and did the next best thing. We let me handle the trial. I was a pre-law major, and even though I was only a freshman, I had watched a lot of Perry Mason. I went to the library, read about the punishment for expired inspection stickers, and discovered that it was rare for anyone to get arrested. This was especially true if the sticker had just expired. This was going to be the crux of our defense.

When it was time to appear in court, I was ready. I took the most legal looking briefcase I had and filled it with books having nothing to do with the law. Since I didn't have any real legal books, I loaded it with philosophy books and tried to look the part. Wearing a grey herringbone sports jacket with brown elbow patches, I carried a pipe for ornamentation. This was about as legal as I could look. Even though I was only eighteen years old, with less hair on my face than a baby's butt, I was ready to conduct my first trial.

The court was called into session and my brother was sworn in and asked to stand before the judge. I stepped up to the bench as well.

"Your honor, I'm here to represent the defendant." He nodded and told me to proceed.

"This is a case of selective prosecution. The defendant was arrested for having an inspection sticker that had been expired for less than a week. He is a full-time student, taking exams, and didn't remember the expiration date. The officer could have given him a ticket and let him get this taken care of, but Instead of the customary ticket they issue in these cases, he put my client in jail."

The judge banged his gavel and called for the arresting officer. "Is Officer Swinney here? Please come forward and get sworn in."

Officer Swinney was sworn in by the Court Administrator and took a seat next to the judge.

"Officer," the judge said. "You've been accused of treating this defendant differently than you typically treat people accused of this offense. Is that true?"

"No. Your Honor, we treat everybody the same."

"That's good to hear. Does the attorney for the defendant want to ask this witness any questions?"

"Yes, your Honor, I would. Officer Swinney, how long have you worked for the police department?"

He sat back and smiled at the easy question. "I've been an officer for over thirteen years."

"Over that time, how many people have you stopped with an expired inspection sticker?"

"I don't know, but it does happen quite a bit."

"And how do you generally deal with this?"

"It depends," he said.

"Depends on what?" I asked.

"It depends on who it is and how long the sticker is expired."

"Would you say the longer the sticker is expired the worse off a person is?"

"That's right."

"And by the same logic, would you say the shorter the time the sticker has expired the better off the person is?"

"I guess so," the officer replied.

"In the last five years, apart from my client, how many people have you arrested for this offense? I want to remind you that you are still under oath and subject to the penalties for perjury."

The officer looked down at the floor before raising his head and answering, "None."

"Officer, didn't you tell this Court that this offense happens all the time, yet in the last five years the only arrest you've made is my client? Can I ask why you stopped him in the first place?"

"I pulled him over because something didn't look right. He was driving in a car with girls in the back seat, and I wanted to make sure the girls were alright."

"Can you explain that a little more?" I asked.

"I didn't know whether he was holding them against their will."

"What would make you think that? Did you hear them screaming for help?"

"No, but they could have been too scared to say anything."

"Did you speak to them?"

"Yes, I did."

"And did they tell you they went to school together and were going out to the Inferno to hear some music?"

"I think that's what they said."

"So they weren't in any danger, right?"

"How am I supposed to know that before I investigate? When I see a suspicious car with innocent looking girls in the back, it's my job to investigate."

"What about my client makes you think he looked suspicious?"

"I don't know. Why else would they be with him? Plus, something about his face looked familiar."

"I think this has more to do with his skin color and less to do with his looks. The only reason you pulled him over was because he was black. That's why you took him to jail rather than giving him a ticket and letting him get his car inspected during the week. He told you he was a college student, and you didn't care."

"Forgetting your responsibility is no excuse for breaking the law."

"I agree, but my client had no criminal record, has no driving violations, and is putting himself through college. Isn't this the kind of person you generally give a break to?"

"If he lived here maybe I would have given him a break, but he's from out of town and I couldn't let him drive a potentially unsafe vehicle on our streets."

"Your honor, I don't have any more questions for this witness. Let me sum up my case. My client was pulled over because Officer Swinney thought his car looked suspicious because he saw some girls in the car who he thought might be in trouble. He spoke to the girls and found out they were all students going out for a night of fun. Instead of giving my client a ticket and requesting he get his car inspected, they took him to jail. I'm sure if I went through the records, I could find hundreds of people who got tickets and didn't live here. As I said in my opening remarks, this is a case of selective persecution, and the answers given by Officer Swinney confirmed the veracity of my remarks. Based on that, I move the case against my client be dismissed."

"Counselor, you've made a very persuasive case. I haven't seen you in this court before. What's your name?"

"Norman Stuart."

"Are you related to the defendant?"

"Yes. He's my brother, and I was in the car when this happened."

The judge looked at me again and asked, "Are you a lawyer?"

"No. I'm a pre-law major at the University.

"You have a bright future if you keep up your studies. Meanwhile, I'm dismissing this case on the grounds presented by defense counsel. I'm also ordering the return of any bail posted."

"Thank you. We appreciate your assistance."

I felt good about winning my first trial but felt bad I couldn't discuss in greater detail the real reasons my brother was taken to jail. It had nothing to do with the inspection sticker and everything to do with us driving in a neighborhood where the darkest thing the police ever saw was their coffee before the milk went in. As far as they were concerned, we were way off the reservation, and it was their job to put us back. For us it was a matter of proving we had a right to go wherever we wanted. It was a revolutionary act to affirm that we didn't have a reservation to be confined to. We went to the same places as everybody else and did the same things other kids our age did. But Officer Swinney reminded us that we couldn't always do the same things as our peers. We were different, and nothing was going to change that. The real reason my brother spent the night in jail was because we were driving with white girls in the car.

The Terminal

It was going to be the world's largest bingo game on national television that night. In front of an audience of millions, Secretary of Defense Melvin Laird would determine who would live and who would die. He would pick numbers to see which lucky men would win all-expense paid trips to the rice paddies of Southeast Asia. Most men in the country between the ages of 18 and 35 were eligible for the drawing. My roommates and I were nervous as we sat there and waited. Though many of our friends were having lottery parties, we wanted to watch the big show at home.

I lit a stick of incense, crossed the room, and put on the album *VOLUNTEERS* by the Jefferson Airplane.

"Are you guys ready," I shouted down the stairs.

While I opened the bottle of Mateus, Mike and Al, two of my roommates, upon hearing Grace Slick's voice, and smelling the incense wafting down the stairs, came up to the living room. Everyone's eyes were focused on the black and white television sitting on the small brown table. Behind it was a poster of Che Guevara, thumb-tacked to a poorly papered wall. On the other wall was a poster advertising the Woodstock Rock Festival that had taken place a few months earlier. None of us were interested in being forced to join the military. We liked our lives as they were and weren't interested in any changes. College, after all, was the one place where we could be irresponsible and feel like we were accomplishing something at the same time.

Mike poured the wine while Al lit a joint the size of a banana. He started passing it around the room while we all sat on the floor, preparing to watch our destinies become determined by a game of chance.

Our other roommate, Ron, who was not part of the party, came into the room, drinking a can of Budweiser. He took a seat on the other side of the room, opened the window, and stuck his head out to take a deep breath.

"Did they start picking the numbers yet?" Jeff asked.

"Not yet," I replied. "Just a lot of bullshit from Nixon!"

Ron replied, "Why don't you guys leave Nixon alone? We're fighting to preserve democracy."

Al jumped in. "I'd like to go to Mississippi and enjoy some of that democracy."

After commercials for Alka Seltzer and Wrigley's spearmint gum, Secretary Laird spun a wire cage containing 365 slips of paper, one slip for every day of the year. Those numbers determined who would get drafted and who could continue their education. As he prepared to pick the first number, you could hear a pin drop on our wine stained rug. Secretary Laird went through the first fifty numbers, and up to that point, we were all safe. We breathed a collective sigh of relief and watched four annoying cigarette commercials.

Secretary Laird resumed pulling numbers and pulled out the number 64, the slip containing my birth date.

I screamed out, "There's no way I'm giving up my life to fight in Nixon's war!"

Mike, ever the optimist, put his arm around my shoulder and said, "Everybody in the army doesn't die."

I shrugged and said, "It's more than being scared of dying. I don't like the type of person you have to become to survive in that reality. Each step you take could be your last, and every time you lay your head down, you have no way of knowing whether you'll ever pick it back up. Taking a bullet is easy, it's waiting for the bullet that's so hard to do."

The other three guys had better luck and received numbers that guaranteed they would probably not be drafted, but there was no jubilation in the room.

I looked at my pals and said, "What happened to the party?"

I started going to the Draft Resister's League, twice a week for counseling. They counseled people on the legal ramifications of disobeying the Selective Service Act. From New York to Los Angeles, men were forming different levels of resistance. The DRL's phone constantly rang with people requesting information on alternatives to joining the Army. After many discussions with the counselors, I decided to transfer to the University of Toronto and live in Canada. Going to school an extra year and having a degree from a Canadian university was a small price to pay, so I applied for the spring term at U/T.

By December 15th, I hadn't received an acceptance letter and was liable to get inducted at any time. If I didn't show up for induction, I could be picked up by the police, arrested, and still end up in the army. My parents understood my dilemma and respected my right to determine my own destiny. I went to the mailbox every morning at 8:45, looking for my letter.

Lying in bed one morning, hung over from a night of excessive libation, Al woke me up. "Danny, there's a couple of letters for you." He handed me the mail, and I saw the letter I was expecting from the University of Toronto. I was glad to finally have that weight off my shoulders. But, unfortunately, I also had the letter I had dreaded receiving. It was a letter telling me to report to the Western New York Army Induction Center. I was going to be fitted for an army uniform even though green wasn't my favorite color.

Finals for the semester were over, and I didn't have a lot of time before my legal status would be changing. So I tied up most of my loose ends and spent as much time as possible visiting friends and family.

I spent my last weekend visiting my family to say goodbye. My father couldn't understand why I was leaving. My sister Veronica flew in from Chicago, taking a week's vacation from her job as a Social Worker. My brother Phil came up from Trenton, where he worked as a pharmaceutical sales rep. We all gathered at the family home in Spring Valley.

"I don't know why you think you have to run away from your responsibility," my father lectured.

"I don't consider fighting in Southeast Asia my responsibility," I replied.

"If the government needs you to fight, then it's your responsibility to go. If people acted like you during World War II, we might all be speaking German now."

My sister Veronica jumped in. "That was different. We were fighting against people trying to subjugate the world. Viet Nam isn't looking to do that."

My father quickly replied, "No, but communism is. It's the same thing. We have to stop them over there before they get over here."

I jumped to my own defense. "Communism is an economic system, and I don't know if you can fight ideas with bullets. I don't want to join the army because I'll have to give up control of my life."

"What do you mean?" My mother asked.

"You have to do what you're told. What if you get sent on a stupid suicide mission? Am I supposed to die for that? What if they tell you to shoot up a village of women and children? Will I be able to live with myself?"

"Son, the Army isn't all bad. I owe everything I have to the Army. They gave me a loan for my first house, which I later used as collateral to start the business. None of that would have been possible without the Army."

"Have you thought about the fact that you won't be able to come back? Think of all the important events you are going to miss," my mother said. "Weddings and funerals, to name a couple."

"You're right, but I have to do what I think is right for me, and right now, that's moving to Canada."

"That means you can't be the Best Man at my wedding next year. Now I have to find somebody to take your place." My brother continued. "Plus, how are you going to support yourself up there? You may have a hard time finding decent work."

"I'm worried you're going to have a hard time finding work, and then you'll be hungry and unable to eat well. You know food is more expensive up there." My mother reached out and grabbed my arm.

"I know. You all have made good points, but I didn't come here to argue about whether I'm doing the right thing or not. I came to say goodbye until I see you again. I want to spend the rest of our time talking about all of the great memories we've shared. That's what's important to me right now."

We spent the rest of the evening talking about everything from childhood to adolescence, and one by one everybody retired to their rooms for the night. After breakfast, I hugged and kissed everybody, told them I loved them, and then took the bus back home.

The last bus to Toronto that next evening was scheduled to leave at 5:30 PM. It was already twelve minutes after five when I rushed into the bank to close my account. Two blocks from the Greyhound bus station, I had just enough time to catch my bus. I searched for the shortest line, but they all were long because it was Friday, and everyone wanted to have cash for the weekend. Finally, I spotted one line with only four people and jumped on the end before someone else did. I prayed no one got involved in any long complicated transactions as the clock kept ticking. Two of the people were together and only deposited a check into their account. The next two people cashed payroll checks and were out of the bank in less than two minutes, but the next customer was a commercial client who had his day's receipts to deposit. He was putting money in different accounts and cutting into my time. He finished, and I walked up to the teller's window, handed her my passbook, and declared my intention to close the account. She took the passbook, checked my ID, and gave me the balance of money in my account. She then stamped the passbook with big red letters ***ACCOUNT CLOSED***.

I put the money in a sock in my duffel bag and had eleven minutes before my bus was leaving. Eleven minutes to leave the bank, run two blocks, buy a ticket, and get on the bus. I rushed out of the bank, with my duffel bag slung over my shoulder, briefly stopping at the traffic light on the corner. My watch now said 5:20, and I wiped the sweat from my forehead. Two trucks and a police car passed before

I dashed across the street, with no plans of stopping until I reached the Greyhound ticket window.

At 5:23 PM, I arrived at the station, panting and out of breath. I bought a ticket to Toronto, put it in my pocket, and prepared to board the bus. Before I could reach the bus platform, I was grabbed by a police officer and told he wanted to ask me some questions. The other officer informed me I didn't have to answer any questions without a lawyer. His partner gave him a nasty look and told him to shut up.

"I'll take care of this while you go call for priors," the first officer hollered. His partner took my college ID card and walked to the police car to call for any criminal history. I was then marched out the back of the station to an alley lined with garbage dumpsters.

I was alone with officer Cochon in the alley behind the bus terminal and asked him, "Why are you detaining me?"

"We had a call about a bank,"

"You're going to make me miss my bus!" I exclaimed.

"I wouldn't be worrying about the bus. What's in the bag?"

"Just my clothes and a little spending money. Let me show you," I responded.

The officer screamed, "Don't you move your hands unless I tell you! And leave that bag on the ground."

I couldn't believe what was going on. I was standing in a dingy, urine stenched alley, for doing nothing more than hurrying to catch a bus.

Now I understood why it was necessary for me to get on the bus. I wouldn't have to deal with things like this. I could walk down the street without causing suspicion. I thought about how good it would feel to be on that bus and leaving this nightmare behind when the policeman discovered the money in my bag.

"You call this a little spending money?"

I turned around to explain when the officer slapped me with the back of his hand. The large ring on his finger tore a cut on my lower lip. He then poured the other contents of my bag onto the ground. I tried to tell him that I had gotten the money from my savings account. "My passbook is right here!" I took my hands from the back of my head, reached into the inside pocket of my coat, and pulled out my passbook.

Before I could show the officer my passbook, a loud shot then rang out. I screamed at the officer and asked, "What are you doing!" I staggered back and fell to the ground. I looked at the smoke coming from his gun and thought it was ironic that instead of dying in a jungle in Southeast Asia, my life was ending in an asphalt jungle in upstate New York. As the life departed from my body, I thought about the people I would never see and the things I would never do. Whenever anyone dies, they always leave tasks undone and words unsaid. Few people, except suicides, make an appointment to meet the grim reaper.

Upon hearing the shot, the other officer rushed over and saw my body lying in a pool of blood.

His partner calmly put his gun back in the holster and said, "I think he robbed the bank across the street, and I thought he was reaching for a gun."

The rookie walked over to my body and took the object I was holding out of my hand. It was a passbook from the bank showing a withdrawal of slightly more than two thousand dollars, stamped in large red letters saying **ACCOUNT CLOSED.**

Pound for Pound

The bright red numbers were staring at me and all I could do was stand there in disbelief. Dumfounded, and too shocked to get off the scale, I had finally become a figment of my own reality. A reality of piling on thousands of calories in some of New York's best restaurants, often staying at the bar until closing, and still finding the energy to drag my alcohol saturated carcass to work the next day. While I was enjoying this high style of living, the only situps I ever did were on the edge of the bar stool, and the only pushups involved pushing myself out of my seat after last call. I might not have been aware of it, but those were not the kinds of activities that kept you in the best physical shape.

In less than two years I had gone from looking like Luke Skywalker to Jabba the Hut, and it wasn't as if my wardrobe hadn't been giving me not so subtle hints. I should have known something was wrong when my belts could no longer make that long journey around my waist. Jackets I had worn for years couldn't be buttoned without the risk of splitting the seams, but I really should have gotten a wake-up call when I had to stop buttoning my shirt collars to keep from strangling myself. It wasn't long before all my suits had to be altered by tailors profiting from my life of hedonistic excess. Instead of taking these signs as warnings of a potential problem, I just figured they weren't making clothes as well as they used to. It wasn't possible that I was getting larger, the dry cleaners were making my clothes smaller.

For most of my adult life I had never weighed more than 160 pounds, but in my current adult state, I was a two-hundred-pound, donut eating heart attack waiting to happen.

The things I hated most about becoming pleasingly plump were the remarks I had to hear from people. "Oh, what happened to you?" Or else I would get those well-wishers who thought they were complimenting my professional success. The worst thing that happened was when my mother's church asked if I could volunteer to be Santa Claus for the annual Christmas pageant.

My girlfriend Camille was giving me one of her sermons about the evils of obesity one evening while we were sitting in her apartment. Camille, a stunningly beautiful woman, spent more than two hours a day in the gym, no less than three times a week. Her idea of a great meal was brown rice topped with steamed organic vegetables. A shade under six feet tall, she had auburn colored skin, dark piercing eyes, and a figure that made men drool. Not only did she love working out, she proselytized about it every chance she got and had been trying to get me to join her gym for the last two years. Camille was the assistant manager of an accounting department she should have been running. After spending two weeks in the hospital a few years ago, she decided to take her health far more seriously than her wealth.

Camille and I had gone to the same high school in Westchester County. She was in my computer science class, and the work was a little easier for me than for her. To my surprise, she stopped me one day after class.

"Do you have a partner for the computer project?" she asked.

"No, I don't," Though we were in the same class and I had seen her around school, this was the first time she had ever spoken to me.

"You seem to be good at that stuff, and I could use some help. I have to get a good grade in this class, or I might not get a scholarship to Brown."

That she wanted to work with me on the project was one of the best things that happened to me that year. Little did I know that twenty years later we would still be friends. What started as a high school friendship turned into what for the last six years has been a close intimate relationship.

Camille won the scholarship to Brown, and I moved to New York and went to NYU. Even though we went to different schools, we stayed in touch.

A few years after college, we both ended up living in Manhattan in the same neighborhood. Ever since that computer class in high school, we have always looked out for each other's best interest, and she had a way of getting me to do what we both knew was right.

"Hey Julian," she said. "They've got a sale on memberships at my gym."

"What are you gonna do, get another lifetime membership?" I joked. "That way if you die and come back, you'll be covered until the middle of the next century."

Camille did not find this as funny as I did. She turned to me and said, "You can laugh if you want, but I want to know when you're going to do something about looking like that." She pointed her finger at my reflection in the mirror.

I knew she was right, but I didn't gain all this weight overnight. It grew on me one pound at a time, and before I knew what was happening, the scale had been moving in the wrong direction. Now I needed to turn things around.

"We're finishing this new program at the bank, and if everything works out, I could be in line for a nice promotion."

"I get it, but you can't spend all your time worrying about a promotion you might never get. The Bank is not worried about you. They just want your labor, and when they finish with you, they'll roll you out and then roll in somebody else."

"I know, but if I don't take advantage of this opportunity, somebody else will."

"If you don't take that first step to getting healthy, you're always going to be too busy. If it's not one thing, it will always be something else. For a guy thirty-six, under six feet tall, you're carrying way too much ham on your bones."

"I can get rid of this any time I want."

"You say that, but if you could do something about looking like that, you would."

"When I'm ready to do something, I will."

"Talk is cheap," Camille said, not letting go of the conversation.

"What do you mean, talk?"

"I'll bet you anything you can't lose that excess belly bulge. I hate to tell you, but if you don't do something, you might be carrying it around for the rest of your abbreviated life. And I'd like you to be around a lot longer than that."

"You think I can't get rid of this?" I said, holding in my stomach, "What do you want to lose? Money, virtue, or how about a little of both?"

"It's your stomach, what can you afford to lose?"

"If I win, you pay for a vacation for the two of us to the Caribbean island of my choice and do any wild and kinky thing I want."

Camille and I were going on vacation anyway, so I would be no worse off if I lost.

"And if I win, you're going to pay for me and my sister Bernice to go to Jamaica to visit my grandmother, and you get to pay for everything, including our non-duty-free shopping spree."

I thought about it and tried to calculate my financial exposure. Based on my calculations, I took the bet and figured I'd do whatever I needed to win. "OK, you've got a deal." I reached over and gave her a big kiss. "Now, what's the bet?"

"Since you're forty pounds overweight, you should lose it in four months." Thinking more like an accountant than a nutritionist, Camille sat back and continued. "That's only ten pounds a month, or two and a half pounds a week."

My only hope was to argue with her math. "I'm only twenty pounds overweight, and I should get six months to lose it."

"You were twenty pounds overweight twenty pounds ago, but I'm gonna make it easy on you. All you have to lose is thirty pounds in six months. That's less than a pound and a half a week. Do you think you can handle that?"

I was getting irritated by her condescending tone, but I knew she was trying to motivate me, and her math made losing the weight seem easy. I should be able to lose a pound and a half a week. Cutting out two trips a week to Burger King should take care of that. "Like I said, you're on! Make sure you have your bank account ready this summer."

"I'm not worried," she said. "There's one more thing."

"What's that?" I asked, stroking my chin, trying to figure out what she was trying to add to the bet.

"We're not having any sex until you've lost at least fifteen pounds."

"What does sex have to do with this?" I protested halfheartedly. It's not like I was setting any marathon sex records lately. I was always too stuffed to do too much more than roll on and fall off a few minutes later. If it wasn't for the fact that she loved me and wanted to see me get better, she would have been gone a long time ago.

"That's the least I can do to help motivate you."

The only reason I ever agreed to such an outlandish deal was because I never figured I would have to pay. If I had to starve myself halfway to death, I was not paying for Camille and her sister to go to Jamaica. I didn't know whether it was the promise of unbridled eroticism in an exotic setting or the fear of presenting Camille and her sister a blank check that motivated me the most, but I was going to have to shed thirty big ones, or lose three thousand little ones. Time being of the essence, I wasted little of it getting on the phone comparing prices and services at every health club in Manhattan. The best clubs were charging over a thousand dollars a year, which was cheap compared to Camille's sister, but I found out that calling clubs and joining them were two different activities.

One month had gone by and I was still letting my fingers do more walking than my feet. Meanwhile, during the month I was calling, I hadn't done one situp, and that pound-and-a-half weekly weight loss program hadn't kicked in yet. As a matter of fact, not only did I not lose any weight, I actually gained three pounds. So Camille figured she'd already won the bet and started calling travel agencies requesting flight information to Jamaica.

I looked at her and halfheartedly laughed. "I don't know why you're asking for that. You're not going to Jamaica on my dime."

"I'm already one sixth of the way there. You keep calling health clubs trying to save twenty-two cents a month, and I'll be eating rasta pasta before you can squeeze the jelly out of a donut."

Things were not looking good for me. I hadn't had any sex in a month and hadn't made a dent in losing the fifteen pounds that could get me some. Sitting home, drinking a beer, and working my way through a bag of potato chips, a commercial for this nationwide health club chain came on the television. Sandwiched in between ads for launching an exciting career as an air conditioning repairman, and another for learning to drive tractor trailers, the health club was having a special promotion that was expiring in two days. Compared to the rates at all the other clubs I had called, this seemed like the bargain I had been searching for. I called the 800 number on the screen and made an appointment to visit one of their clubs located a couple of blocks from my office. After briefly inspecting the facility, I signed up for a three-year membership, and was now committed to not paying for Camille's trip. My only problem now was that I still had to lose over thirty pounds, and only had five months left to do it.

TJ's Body Shop was located in midtown Manhattan near Madison Avenue and the swanky boutiques frequented by women who shopped with chauffeurs waiting in their cars. Located a few blocks from the Plaza Hotel, it was surrounded by some of the most impressive office towers in New York. Situated amidst East Side splendor, it was a relatively small gym that offered few amenities. If you were looking for comfort, this was not your kind of place, because you always had to wait in lines to use the equipment. Exercise classes required reservations two days in advance, and if you came to the gym after work on a Monday or Tuesday, you had to wait fifteen minutes to get a locker. When you finally got one, it was usually too small to hold a business suit and gym bag. When you finished working out, your suit was so wrinkled it looked more like something you slept in than what you wore to work. I found out a little later that the security guards were illegally renting out the best lockers, and that was why they were always unavailable. Of course, none of these things were included in the smooth-talking sales pitch I got when I initially signed up.

Before I was allowed to work out, I had to go through an orientation where my measurements were taken in order to put me on a program specifically designed to help me achieve my fitness goals. The two people I took orientation with looked like they didn't need to be in the gym. One woman visiting New York wanted to firm up before going home. She couldn't have weighed more than a hundred pounds in the rain. The other guy had a 28-inch waist, weighed 155 pounds, and compared to me, looked like he had a negative percentage of body fat.

Meanwhile, when the trainer took my measurements, my waist rang in at a whopping 39 and a half inches, and the body analysis said that over 30 percent of my body was useless fat cells. I was so embarrassed I put my head down and hoped no one standing around me had heard him. Though we were all at different levels of fitness, we were given the same program to fix our vastly different needs. I didn't usually agree with one-size-fits-all philosophies, but looking at myself in the mirror, I was in no position to object.

My program consisted of riding a stationary bicycle for ten minutes, doing a series of weight training exercises for a half hour, and then riding the bike for another twenty minutes. We were told if we did this three times a week, we could see results in a few months. I asked the session trainer how many months, because I only had five to play with. He looked at me, then he looked at the statistics he had written on my card, and said losing thirty pounds in five months was going to be hard, but not impossible. Not impossible were now the words that became my new marching orders.

The main reason I chose TJ's was because I didn't want my gym to be a social outlet. What I needed was a no-nonsense place where I could focus on losing the weight I needed to get rid of.

TJ's East had two levels, with a swimming pool and jacuzzi on the lower level, while the upper level had the exercise room with all the weightlifting machines and cardio equipment. Twenty bicycles occupied one side of the room, while eight breath sucking stairmasters resided along an adjacent mirrored wall. When the air conditioning wasn't working, which was often, the sweat would drip from people's bodies so profusely the machines had to be wiped off after every use. Eventually, the sweat problem became so bad the club mandated everyone carry a towel or not be allowed to work out. Of course, you could always rent a towel from the club for a dollar.

The rust-stained ceiling tiles often leaked water. Black industrial carpeting, well-worn in front of the popular exercise stations, covered the floor, and unlike the chlorine smell that permeated the lower level, the upper level had the funky scent of a used tennis shoe.

Another section of the gym held aerobics classes, with blaring music and people hopping and jumping, trying to keep up with the instructor. Those in the front lines matched the instructor step for step, while the people in the back were relative newcomers struggling to learn the steps. Moving like a Radio City chorus line, the people in the front would scream in ecstasy each time they reached an aerobic climax.

Behind the aerobics floor were the free weights and powerlifting machines. There was no room for featherweights here. These people did not come to the gym for light stuff. They were there for blood and guts iron pumping. Sometimes I thought these guys were hired by the club to make everyone else look bad, and motivated to work harder. They walked around modeling the latest gym wear and hitting on different men or women.

Another group of people I came to recognize were the personal trainers looking for clients. They hung around the orientation classes and always knew who the new members were. First, they'd come up and give you pointers on how to properly use the equipment, before making the pitch about how much more you could progress with them as your trainer. If you didn't sign up, that was the end of any free pointers.

After a month of doing the program, I had lost ten pounds and was feeling pretty good. Though feeling good emotionally, I'd be lying if I said I was feeling good physically. I was tired and sore almost every day. Exercising muscles that had been dormant for years, I would sit at work for hours, aching, and spaced out in pain. Down to 185 pounds, I had twenty more to go, and four months to do it. This was not going to be easy, but not as impossible as I first thought.

I maintained the same level of exercise for the next few weeks, unable to get my weight below 180. Reaching this impasse, I turned up the heat. I stopped drinking beer, slowed down the fast food, and put a freeze on the ice cream. I then started going to the gym four times a week and taped a picture of how I used to look on my refrigerator for extra motivation.

After a few weeks of this increase in exercise, the fat cells started melting again. For the first time in over two years, I was below 180 pounds. My loose-fitting clothes became a testament to my effort. I could button suit jackets without overburdening the seams. I no longer had to unfasten my pants after big meals, and I could even button the top collar of my old shirts without pinching my neck. I was so encouraged I increased the workouts to five times a week, and rarely saw any of my friends. My relatives didn't hear from me, and I wasn't concerned about the sex I wasn't getting. I was too tired to do anything anyway. This bothered one of my best friends, Mike, came over to my apartment to see why no one saw me anymore.

"Hey Julian, what's going on? Where have you been hiding?"

"I've been spending a lot of time getting myself back into shape. I've got this bet with Camille, and I still have ways to go."

"You look great," Mike said. He looked at me and shook his head. "You make me want to get back into the gym. I could afford to lose a couple of pounds."

"I'll tell you what," I told him. "After I finish this bet with Camille, we'll get some tickets and go see the Knicks. It'll be my treat."

"That works for me."

With two months and fifteen more pounds to lose, the weight was no longer being cooperative. Even though I was sweating buckets and pushing my muscles until they burned, I was not losing weight as fast as when I first started. The weightlifting was helping to build more muscles. My posture was more upright, and I spent more time looking at myself in the mirror, but I still needed to lose fifteen more pounds. I started running four miles every Saturday morning.

It was hard to believe that only a few months earlier I was eating donuts and drinking multiple cups of coffee for breakfast. Now, when I met my friends for dinner, I was drinking spring water, and eating salads and pasta instead of steak and potatoes.

With less than four weeks to go I was still eight pounds over my goal. My daily workouts were lasting over three hours, and my lunches were no longer coming from restaurants. I was actually going to the supermarket and getting food from the salad bar. I would drag my aching muscles to the Food Emporium on Second Avenue, get on the line around the salad bar, and fill my plastic tin with the same ingredients every day, a bed of lettuce, some gazpacho vegetables, chickpeas, and a tiny scoop of tuna. In another container I would fill it with some fruit salad without the syrup. I also traded in my Coca Cola's for small bottles of water.

Even if I didn't lose the thirty pounds at the end of the six months, I felt so good that no matter what it cost, it was worth it. I had my body back. As much as I used to tease Camille about living in the gym, I was spending more time there than she did, and the next time I stepped on the scale, I was one pound under my goal, 164 pounds of joy and happiness. I called Camille.

"Hey Camille, guess what?"

"Surprise me!"

"I'm getting some travel brochures to Aruba and St. Maarten. My scale says I get to pick one at your expense."

"There's still two weeks left for you to find your way back to McDonald's."

"I can do that after I win."

Now under my target weight, I started forgetting which song had brought me to the dance. Bored with living in the gym the past few months, I started going there less and going out after work more. It felt good not being under the enormous stress of *not having a life*. I even splurged and had a thick tenderloin or two, with baked potatoes drowning in butter and sour cream. Three days before the end of the contest, the scale started moving in the wrong direction, and I ballooned up to 168 pounds. I rushed back to TJ's and went on a suicide diet. After three days of drinking carrot juice and riding the exercise bike, I was back to 163 pounds, and ready to call Camille with the good news for my resurrected libido and the bad news for her bank account. Instead of calling, I ran over to her apartment to let her see my weight on her scale.

"I know you didn't think I could do it," I told her.

"I didn't say you couldn't do it. I said you wouldn't do it. The way you started, I actually thought you were going to quit months ago."

"You know me better than that. I would have done anything short of cheating to win."

"I counted on that. You may have won the bet, but look at what you had to do to win. As far as I'm concerned, I won the larger bet we never wagered. To see how hard you worked to get yourself back into shape is worth every penny I'm going to spend."

"If you look at it that way, I guess we both won," I admitted.

Reaching into my leather briefcase, I pulled out a manilla envelope filled with travel brochures and asked Camille if she preferred Aruba to St. Maarten. She started looking at the brochures while I thought about all the crazy things we could do on a wild Caribbean vacation. This would also give me the opportunity to think about how I was going to integrate my old lifestyle into my new one.

Springing Forth

I was on my way to Chicago to be on national television, and I was sure every TV in my hometown of Crimson Creek, Mississippi, would be watching. People all over the world were going to see me make my television debut. With any luck, I could become famous. I had a lot of things on my mind that morning while I struggled through the rush hour traffic. At this time of day, it was going to take another twenty minutes to get to the airport.

When I got the call from one of the producers of the show, I thought it was a practical joke from one of the guys I worked with at the gas station. But much to my surprise, everything turned out to be legit. I was told that I was being brought to the show because somebody I knew wanted to tell me something. I had no idea who it was, or what they wanted to tell me, but for a free trip to Chicago, I'd listen to damn near anything.

I pulled into the visitor's lot and parked at my pre-assigned space. Picking up my boarding pass, I waited for a small plane taking me to Nashville, where I would board another plane headed to Chicago.

This was my first time traveling outside of the state. I'd been almost everywhere in the state, but never ventured outside the Mississippi borderline. On the first plane, I sat up front.

"Mr. Johnson, can I get you something to drink?" the flight attendant asked.

"I'll take a beer, if you got one."

"I think we can get that for you. Would you like some peanuts to go with that beer? So, are you staying in Memphis, or are you heading somewhere else?" the attendant asked.

"I'm going to Chicago to be on television."

"Are you an actor?"

"Not really. I'm gonna be on this show because somebody I know wants to tell me something."

"Couldn't they just tell you on the phone?"

"If they did that then I wouldn't get the free trip."

"I see your point," she said. "You're going to find out what they want to tell you anyway, so you might as well get a free trip out of it."

"That's exactly what I was thinking."

"Let me go get you that beer and an extra bag of peanuts."

On the next plane, I got the VIP treatment with more beer, a ham sandwich, and a jumbo bag of potato chips.

When the plane landed, I got off and saw a lady holding a sign with the name Billy Ray Johnson on it. I walked over and introduced myself.

"I'm Billy Ray Johnson."

"Hi Billy Ray. My name is Cynthia Chadbourn. I'm the Producer of the show *My Big Surprise*. We're happy you could make it and want you to have a good time while you're here. If there is any way I can make your stay here better, please let me know."

"I appreciate that, Cynthia. What are we gonna do now?"

"I'm going to take you to your hotel and let you freshen up."

"That sounds good, but I still want to know why I'm here?"

"That's because someone you either know now, or knew in your past, wants to tell you something."

"Couldn't they just tell me on the phone and save all this money?"

"Telling people something face to face is always better than writing a letter or making a phone call. Don't you agree?"

"I guess so, but can you at least tell me who it is?"

"That'll spoil *The Big Surprise*. You'll find out soon enough."

"As long as it ain't a surprise baby, and somebody looking for back child support, I'm OK."

Since she wasn't going to say who wanted to tell me something, I figured it had to be an old girlfriend. I was pulling out what little hair I had left, trying to figure out who it could be.

"I don't know Billy Ray. Meanwhile, here's a voucher for you to eat at the restaurant across the street from your hotel."

"How's the food?"

"We send all our guests there, and nobody's complained yet."

"That's good to hear."

Cynthia gave me a voucher for a restaurant called The Outback Steak House. Though I had never eaten Australian food, this steak was so good I ordered another one to take back to my room.

That next morning, I met Cynthia for coffee and to talk about the show. We walked into the Green Room and were met by the team of security guards. They were so big they made my high school football team look like girl scouts.

"Billy Ray, I'm Paul Stevens and I'm the head of security. I want to go over some ground rules with you."

"Nice meeting you."

"Let me introduce you to my guys over here. "That's Jim, Todd, Bill, and Melvin. Things can sometimes get a little out of control, and if they give you an order, you have to follow it. We don't want anyone getting hurt. Even if you get provoked, we want you to keep your cool. It's OK to wrestle around a little, or do some pushing and shoving, but we don't want any bona fide ass kicking. Is that clear? This is for ratings and not revenge."

"I get it. You want us to pretend fight?"

"Yeah, that's right Billy Ray. You pretend to be fighting to give the crowd something to scream about."

"It's Ok as long as I ain't the one gettin' my ass whipped." I poured a cup of coffee and put two donuts on a paper plate. I sat down, turned towards Cynthia, and said, "I still can't figure out who wants to tell me something."

"All I can say is that someone you are connected to has something to tell you."

"That's the same thing you said before."

"That's right. You're going to find out in less than an hour, so why don't you go have another donut?"

This was a brain teaser. I could not for the life of me guess who might want to tell me something in Chicago they couldn't tell me back home.

"And you're sure it's my girlfriend who wants to tell me this?"

"I didn't say that. It could also be somebody associated with her."

"I guess I'm just gonna wait and see what happens."

When they called me to the stage, I saw my girlfriend's ex-husband, Buddy Harwell, sitting in a chair in the center of the stage. I heard he had just gotten out of jail for stealing two cases of beer and a bag of barbecue chips. The Judge gave him eighteen months in the County Jail since this was his second offense. His wife Lily filed for divorce two weeks later. Buddy looked over at me and said, "I know you been messin' with my wife, ever since I went to jail. I brought you here to tell you to back off and let me get back together with her."

"First of all, I was messin' with your wife before you went to jail, and she doesn't want to be with you, so I got no reason to back off."

"Unless I get papers sayin' otherwise, she's still my wife, and I ain't gonna have you sleeping with her."

"She's moving into my place next month, and there ain't a damn thing you can do about it."

"Not if I can help it." Buddy got up from his seat and walked across the stage towards my chair. I got up to see what he was going to do. "I'm gonna do something about it." He rushed at me, mostly slapping air, and I threw my share of wayward punches that never landed. The security guards finally rushed in and separated us. The crowd cheered like they were at the Roman Coliseum rooting for the lions.

Buddy grew up in Crimson Creek, lived around the corner from me, and we attended the same schools. We had our share of tussles growing up, and I always came out on top, but that never stopped him from trying again.

The host interceded and asked, "Let me ask you something Billy Ray. If she's still his wife, why are you messing with her?"

"She doesn't want to be with him. She's divorcing him and starting a new life."

"Well Buddy, what do you have to say about that?"

"She don't want me 'cause he's interfering with everything."

"Jerry, he treats the hogs on his daddy's farm better than her. Last year he made her give him money to get her a Christmas present. He spent most of the last two years in jail, and if he loved her, he'd treat her better than that."

"What about that Buddy?"

"Some of what he says might be true, but I'm fixin' to change."

I cut in before he could get another word out. "What don't you understand? She doesn't want anything to do with you, and those divorce papers should be hitting your mailbox any day now. You had your chance, and you blew it."

"What does she tell you?" Jerry asked Buddy. "Does she say she wants to be with you?"

"Not exactly, but if he wasn't interfering with my marriage, she might be looking to get back with me."

"You don't have a marriage, you idiot." I walked over to him and pointed a finger in his face. "It's about time you moved on."

"Alright. No hard feelings." Buddy reached out to shake my hand. I went to shake his hand, and instead of shaking hands, he threw an uppercut and hit me in the stomach. I didn't care what the security guards said, I wasn't letting him get away with sucker punching me on national TV. We tussled around on stage with no one really connecting any serious blows. The security guards finally separated us and took us to opposite ends of the stage.

Jerry turned to the audience and said, "Let's see what Lily has to say about this. Let's welcome Lily to the stage."

The crowd clapped, Buddy's ex-wife and my current girlfriend, Lily Mae Jefferson, walked out onto the stage. She said hello to Jerry and took a seat. I walked over and gave her a big fat sloppy kiss, which further infuriated Buddy. He started to charge at me again, but the security guards held him back.

"See what I mean Jerry. He's kissin' my wife right in front of my face. The way I was brought up, you never let a man kiss your wife, except on Christmas."

"Buddy, when are you gonna get it through your thick skull that I have no love for you?" Lily sat there exasperated, with her arms folded and a look of disbelief on her face.

"You used to love me."

"I guess everybody's entitled to make a mistake or two in life, but it's time for you to get a new life."

"I don't want a new life. I want my old one back."

"That life is over. I should have never married you in the first place. I made a mistake and like my grandma always said, "There ain't nothing wrong with making a mistake, but you're a damn fool if you repeat it.""

"You dirty whore. You been commitin' adultery on our sacred wedding vows, and you call me a mistake?"

Buddy jumped out of his seat and walked over to me, pointing his finger. "It's all your fault. You been filling her head with all this bullshit."

"Buddy, if you're trying to get back with Lily, calling her a whore on national TV is probably not going to help your case," Jerry told him.

Lily looked up at him and said, "Jerry, now you see why I'm done with him. He doesn't respect me. I just want to move on, without him."

Jerry turned to Buddy and said, "What do you want to say about that? She wants to move on with her life and wants you to accept that."

"I'll never accept that. Not till the day I die."

The host gave his final remarks to the audience and thanked us for sharing our stories. Three separate cabs were waiting to take us to the airport. All the way home I thought about what people were gonna say about Buddy sucker-punching me. Should I have kicked his ass no matter what I promised the security team? Buddy made a fool of me in front of the whole world, and I had to live with that.

The flight home couldn't land fast enough. I was mad, but glad Lily told Buddy in front of the world that she wanted nothing to do with him. I got off the plane and walked to the lot to get my truck. I fished my keys out of my bag and turned 3waround. Walking out of the terminal towards his truck, I saw Buddy Harwell, and there were no security guards to stop me. He got away with sucker-punching me in Chicago, but now I set out to give him an ass whipping of biblical proportion.

Get out of the Rain

It was 3:30, the plane had been circling for over an hour, and I wondered whether it was ever going to land. The fog was so thick you could cut it with a plastic knife, and it prevented me from seeing anything on the ground. I had hoped this was not an omen.

This was the first time I had visited Germany. Though I looked more like my African-American father, I was as much German as I was American. Because my mother was born in Dusseldorf. Though most of her early memories were fond, everything changed one unforgettable night.

Her family had been arrested during the war and placed in a rehabilitation camp. They had owned a newspaper and occasionally wrote editorials criticizing the government's burning of books and anti-Semitic persecutions. They couldn't understand how easily most of the newspapers in Germany had allowed themselves to be censored.

My mother had told me the story of visiting a friend and waiting for her brother to give her a ride home. He was fifteen minutes late, which was unusual for him. When she called home, no one picked up the phone, and twenty minutes later, after she called again, the phone still went unanswered. She decided walking would be faster than waiting for her brother. As she walked down her street, two large army trucks sped past, running through a red light, climbing the peak of the avenue, and disappearing. Forty minutes later, she saw the soldiers who had passed her previously, parked in front of her house. She decided not to get any closer until she could figure out what was going on. Hiding behind two large garbage cans, sitting on cold concrete in a new dress, she watched her father and mother be put into the back of one of the trucks. In the other truck, they placed her brother Karl, and her two sisters, Anna and Gretchen. She sat there frozen in fear, wanting to cry but didn't for fear of drawing attention to herself. Her mother, father, two sisters, and brother were being taken to an unspecified place, for an unspecified reason, for an indeterminate length of time. She had no idea that would be the last time she would ever see them.

With the help of friends, Marta was able to sneak into Belgium and escape to Switzerland, where she stayed until the end of the war. It was here where she met my father, who was stationed in the army near Zurich. They became friends, eventually married, and she emigrated to the United States with him after the war.

I couldn't understand why my mother never wanted to return home to see how things had changed. Despite what happened to her family, she shouldn't blame present generations for the sins of the past. I was determined to visit the city where my ancestors once lived.

It was 4:30 when the captain announced they were finally going to land the plane, and I had until 6:00 to get to the hotel before losing my reservation.

After getting off the plane, I followed the green multilingual signs directing incoming passengers to the appropriate Customs station. When I got to the station for non-European citizens, the officials were simply glancing at passports and letting everyone go to the next room to retrieve their baggage. The two lines were moving very quickly when my turn came up. I walked up to a woman wearing a grey wool uniform with a black stripe down the side. Her grey hair was in need of a visit to the beauty parlor, and she wore no lipstick or other makeup to help improve her surly looks. I smiled and handed her my passport. She acted like she wasn't allowed to show any human emotion and started studying my passport as if she suspected it was forged, or in some other way, not legitimate. She kept looking at the picture and staring at my face.

"Why are you visiting Germany?" she asked.

I looked up at her and replied, "I'm here on vacation."

"How long do you plan to be here?"

"About two weeks."

"May I see your plane ticket?"

"They took it when I boarded the plane to get here."

"I want to see your return ticket."

It was bad enough that my plane was two hours late, but to have to show a ticket when I wasn't getting on a plane made no sense. So I asked her, "I'm not getting on a plane, so why do you need to see my ticket?"

"If you don't show me your ticket you will not be permitted into this country."

"I don't see you asking anyone else for their tickets?"

"If you don't believe me, then you should read this. " She handed me a regulation book printed in German. Fighting with this woman wasn't worth the effort, so I relented and handed her the ticket. She studied it like she was taking an exam on its contents and asked me some questions about the ticket's details before finally allowing me to pass.

As soon as I passed, she picked up the phone on the desk behind her counter and made a call. Her face turned bright red while she screamed at some poor soul on the other end of the line. I went to the baggage carousel, got my luggage, and headed for the Customs exit station. When I arrived, the guards requested my passport and asked me to open my bags. They opened and searched my bags, looking into the pockets of my pants, unrolling my underwear, and even turning my socks inside out, leaving nothing in my possession untouched.

It was nearly 5:30, and my hotel reservation was going to expire in thirty minutes. I tried to explain that to the guards and asked if I could make a call, but they wouldn't help me. One of the Customs agents saw me constantly looking at my watch and surmised that I had something to hide. He ordered me to another room and made me empty the contents of my bags onto a large metal table.

Five minutes later, two more officials came into the room. One was wearing a white medical smock and could have been a doctor. He was wearing white rubber gloves and carried a little flashlight, while the other man carried an AK-47 and wore a military police uniform with two pairs of handcuffs hanging around the back of his waist. He did not look like he was having a good day.

"Are you carrying any illegal substances? He asked.

"No," I emphatically told him.

"Can you prove that to us?"

"You can prove it yourself. You guys have all my luggage on the table over there, and you guys already looked through them and didn't find anything."

"Smugglers are very clever. They often hide things on their bodies."

"I'm not a smuggler, and I don't have anything on my body except hair."

"We'll be the judge of that. Can you to take your clothes off and put them on this table next to your clothes?"

I had never been strip searched before and didn't like how this was feeling. I hadn't been in the country five minutes, and I was already in trouble.

My dignity was going down the drain faster than dirty bath water. I hadn't done anything, but was standing naked in a small room at the airport with some guy about to shine a flashlight up my ass.

The taller of the two men walked across the room with the flashlight in his hand and said to me, "Please bend over and touch your toes."

I bent over, barely reaching my toes, while he walked behind me, spread my cheeks, and shined the flashlight up my ass. Next, he shined the flashlight down my throat and in my ears while the police officer rifled through my clothes again.

At 6:30, they told me I could go. I was hoping my hotel reservation wasn't canceled. Unfortunately, I had no change for the telephone, and didn't know how it worked anyway, so I looked for a cab to head straight to the hotel. After twenty minutes of waiting for the taxi, and another twenty-five to get to the hotel, it was 7:15 when I walked up to the reservation desk and asked for my room.

The clerk looked up and asked, "What is your name, sir?"

"Douglas Garadin."

"I'm sorry Mr. Garadin, your reservation has been canceled."

"What do you mean?"

"You were supposed to be here by 6:00, or call to say you'd be late. We didn't hear from you by 7:00 and tried calling you, but no one answered your phone."

"No one answered because I wasn't there. That's because I'm here. My plane was late, and it took me a long time to go through immigration and customs."

"I'm sorry to hear that, but your room was given away, and we have no more left."

"You have no more left?" My voice started getting louder by the word. "Maybe you better go get the manager!"

The manager, hearing the commotion, came out and explained that there was a trade show in town, and it was impossible to keep the room available past the one-hour grace period.

"If you come back Monday," he said, "I'll have a nice room for you, and we won't charge you for the first night.."

"And where am I supposed to sleep until then?"

"I can call another hotel and see if there is room for you. They usually have vacancies."

"OK. As long as it's clean."

The manager made the call, gave me the address, and told me how to get there. With my luggage in hand, I walked out the front door and headed for the Tainput Hotel. It wasn't a long walk, but the hard rain soaked my clothes to the stitches.

I arrived at the Tainput and asked the clerk for a room. He looked up from his newspaper and asked, "How many hours will you need it for?" I thought that was a strange question but didn't pay it any mind.

"I'll need it for the weekend, but maybe longer."

I walked up the stairs, unlocked the door, and entered my new home for the weekend. The small room, with two beds, had a sink and mirror on one end of the room and a bathroom with a shower on the other. A large window faced a six-story office building. The room had a familiar but unidentifiable smell, and the towels and sheets looked like they had been donated by someone cleaning out an ancestor's attic. A small blue rug sat on the floor between the two beds, and a rocking chair faced a small black and white television. I turned on the radio while I unpacked my bags. Besides the music, I heard the rhythmic creaking of an old bed spring. I laughed and wondered who was getting busy in the room.

After unpacking my clothes, I got a quick bite to eat in the hotel restaurant before going to hang out in an area with over two hundred bars and restaurants in a one-half square mile area. Located in the old part of Dusseldorf called *the Altstadt*, there was a bar or restaurant in every building, and people traveled from all over Europe to go bar hopping in this area of 17th and 18th-century buildings, on cobblestone streets.

I went into a small bar, ordered a beer, and fifteen minutes later, I signaled the bartender who had brought me my beer, "Can I ask you something?"

The bartender had a puzzled look on his face and replied, "How can I help?"

"I'm visiting and wanted to ask you about some of the cool places in town. Where can I do a little dancing and drinking, and maybe get lucky, if you know what I mean?"

"If you want to go dancing and maybe get lucky, you should go to Bam/Bam's. It's only five minutes from here."

"Ok. Thanks for the tip."

When I got to Bam/Bam's, I could hear the music all the way out to the street. It was loud and seemed to make the sidewalk shake. I walked down the stairs into the main room, crossed the floor to the bar, and ordered a drink. Though it was still early, the dance floor was already crowded.

I asked a couple of women to dance, but they both turned me down. I watched several people on the floor dancing with themselves. I wasn't ready to do that, but I did dance in place, bopping to the music. Halfway through the song, a tall woman in a yellow leather jumpsuit pulled me out to the dance floor, imitating every dance move I made. The crowd started watching and clapping, with people moving out of the way for me and the lady in the yellow jumpsuit.

When we were too tired to dance anymore, I wiped my forehead and attempted to introduce myself. "My name is Doug."

"My name's Kristine."

"Can I get you something to drink?"

"I'll take whatever you're having."

I ordered two beers, and we sat down at a table.

"Where in America do you live?" she asked.

"I live in New York."

"That's so cool. I always wanted to go there."

"I think you'd like it. Do you live here in town?"

"No, I live in Cologne. I came here with my boyfriend, but we had a big fight and I'm going to go back home."

"I'm sorry to hear that."

"That's OK. I should have left him a long time ago."

"Can I ask you something? Why did you stay if you thought you should have left him?"

"I was scared, but now I don't care."

This could really work to my advantage. She might be ready for some rebound sex, and I may be grabbing the rebound. So I asked Kristine, "What are you doing tomorrow?"

"I don't know," she said. "I had planned to be here for the weekend, but now I don't know." She looked down at the floor when she spoke.

"Why don't you stay anyway? You can show me the town!"

"Let me think about it,"

I backed off a little to let things develop at their own pace. A man wearing a black motorcycle jacket and green camouflage boots walked towards us. He yelled something in German, and she responded just as angrily. She put her arms around me in a way that made him uncomfortable. I didn't need to speak German to know what was going on. I didn't know how I did it, but I managed to get in the middle of a German soap opera. The man turned to Kristine and said, "Is this your new lover?"

Kristine laughed at him and replied, "I just met him!"

"Are you going to bed with him?"

"That's none of your business!"

"I need to talk to you," the man cried to Kristine.

"We've done enough talking," she said. "I don't want to see you anymore!"

"I won't go until you talk to me!" the man said.

"You need to go away," she angrily replied.

Even though Kristine kept asking the man to leave, he refused to go. I leaned over and asked her, "Do you want me to ask him to leave?"

I decided to tell the guy anyway. "The lady said she wants you to leave, so why don't you go?"

"She's my girlfriend, and this is none of your business!"

"You mean ex-girlfriend! She doesn't want to be with you anymore."

Klaus grabbed her arm to take her away. "You better come with me!" he exclaimed. "I promise I won't hit you again."

I jumped in front of him and said, "If you don't take your fucking hands off of her right now, I'm going to kick your ass into the middle of next week. And if you think I can't do it, keep grabbing her."

Klaus let her go and said, "I just want to talk to her."

"That's not how you do it. You have no business putting your hands on her. If you want to punch on somebody, why don't you punch me?"

"I don't want to fight you. I just want Kristine to come back with me."

"How can I trust you?" You could see the hurt in her eyes as she spoke. "You said that before."

"This time is different," he said. "You are the most important person in my life, and I don't want to lose that."

I already had enough problems and the last thing I needed was to be in the middle of a foreign love triangle. Before Klaus left, he said something to Kristine and headed for the door. Before he could reach the exit, she turned to me and said, "I have to go! But it was nice meeting you!" She ran after Klaus, and I saw neither of them again.

After Kristine left, I went back to the hotel to get some sleep. I wondered whether he was going to beat her up again, and my guess was that it was only a matter of time.

This was more than enough excitement for one evening. I walked down the street and noticed for the first time since I was in Germany that it had finally stopped raining. The night was clear, and the stars were shining against the black backdrop of the evening sky. I tried hailing a cab back to the hotel but was passed up three times. I muttered to myself, "If I wanted to get passed up by cabs, I could have stayed home." I stopped trying and walked back to the hotel. My feet were tired, my shirt was wet from the dancing, and I had no idea of what I would hear from my neighbors next door. I figured I had two days before some other impossible situation was hurled in my path. At the rate I was going, the police might raid the hotel and arrest me for being in a place of ill repute.

When I got back to my room, I wasn't waiting for my next surprise. As much as I had wanted to come to Germany, it wasn't what I expected. In one day, I managed to get strip searched at the airport, find lodging in a brothel masquerading as a legitimate hotel, and watched a lady choose an abusive, suicidal knucklehead over me. Another hour of German inhospitality was not on my vacation agenda. I had come to visit the home of my grandparents, but all of the drama I had to deal with kept me from doing any genealogical research. I packed my bags, walked to the train station, and got on a train following the sunshine into the Netherlands.

Fool's Gold

Everybody was talking about the internet. Half of the people I spoke to had no idea what it was, and the other half had no idea how to use it. The main topic of conversation rolling off the lips of all my tech buddies was the World Wide Web. They saw how valuable it could be to leverage information from people anywhere on the planet to help solve technical problems in a fraction of the time it used to take.

My friend Alan was one of the first people I knew taking advantage of this new technology. Though he lived in Brooklyn, he was studying economics from a university in London. That was great for him, but I always thought one of the benefits of going to school was the large pool of potential dating prospects.

Companies doing business online discovered they could sell more goods at lower prices because they didn't have the overhead costs associated with a physical store. The internet had something for everybody. Recipes for homemakers, exercise routines for fitness buffs, and pornography for the sexually depraved.

I had recently broken up with my girlfriend, and finding dates when I was on the rebound never worked well for me. One of my friends told me to investigate internet dating services.

"C'mon Phil," Cathy extolled. "You should give it a chance."

"I don't know. It just doesn't sound right. I'd rather meet somebody at a bar. That way I can see what they look like. Plus, it's hard to get somebody drunk sitting in front of a computer screen."

"You should have been born four thousand years ago, living in the back of a cave."

"To be honest, life was a lot simpler for men then. None of this dating stuff. If you saw a woman you liked, you just picked her up, threw her over your shoulder, and took her home."

"Thank God for women's liberation. If not, you'd still be eating raw meat."

I quipped, "I'm sure we would have invented fire by then and learned how to burn the meat."

"Speaking of throwing women over your shoulder, I have a friend who might be able to help you."

"I. don't think I'm up for any more blind dates."

"She doesn't want to date you. She works at an online dating service and said her clients are ecstatic about the results they've been getting."

"You think I could find somebody online?"

Cathy looked at me and said, "Anything's possible, but you'll never know unless you try. Her company is doing a special this month. They're offering the first month free, and with any luck you might find somebody in the first couple of weeks and not have to pay anything. That's a lot cheaper than your monthly bar tab."

"I'm sure I won't be that lucky. With my luck, I'll end up meeting somebody, get married, and divorced two years later with hefty alimony payments staring me in the face."

Cathy teased, "There's nothing like a positive attitude when you're looking to find love."

The first thing I did after work the next day was to hustle over to the *Can't Go Wrong* dating service. The people working there looked like they belonged on the set of a Hollywood movie. Beautiful women wearing low cut blouses were escorting men back to the interview offices. I sat on a couch that cost more than everything in my apartment and waited for the next associate to interview me.

A tall woman with long red hair, wearing a different shade of the same low-cut blouses all the other women were wearing, came from the back and called for me.

"I'm looking for Phil," she said. "Is there a Philip Johnson here?" she asked.

I stood up and replied, "I'm Philip Johnson."

She walked over and stuck out her hand. "I'm Parker, and I'll be explaining the different services we offer."

We shook hands. "Obviously, you already know I'm Phil Johnson and I'm happy to meet you. I've heard some good things about your company."

"Well, thank you Phil. We're going to walk down to my office, and I'll tell you everything you need to know."

We walked down a narrow hall, passing a small kitchen and a set of his-and-her bathrooms. Parker's office was in the corner of the building. A large desk occupied one wall with a small round table and two chairs sitting in the middle of the room. I sat in the chair facing the door while Parker sat in the other.

"Can I offer you something to drink?" she asked, with an accent nurtured in the southern part of the country. "I don't know about you, but I could sure use a glass of wine."

"That sounds good to me."

Parker walked over to her desk, pulled two glasses from the bottom drawer, and filled them with the wine. We clinked glasses and said cheers.

Parker put her glass down and asked. "Are you ready to find out why you can't go wrong here?"

"I guess I'm as ready as I'll ever be."

"First, I want to welcome you to our office. As a member, you can come here anytime we're open and use our computers. There's always plenty of people hanging around, and there's always snacks in the fridge."

"That's good to know."

"Here's how everything works. First, we take the information you provided on your application and feed it to our computer. It looks at your profile and the profiles of thousands of women who match the criteria you stipulated. Then we give you a list of the top ten matches, and you're then free to contact them and see where everything goes."

"How much is this going to cost?" I asked.

Parker crossed her legs and smiled. "That depends on which plan you choose."

"Can you give me an idea?"

"Sure. If you want to meet non-Ivy League college graduates and come to our monthly social, it will cost you $150 per month billed in 90-day increments."

"I'm going to assume if I wanted the package to include Ivy League women, it would be more."

"Well, don't you pay more for a BMW than a Hyundai?"

"Yes, but by the sale logic, if I was only interested in high school graduates, then the fee would be less."

"Theoretically, yes, but we don't work with high school graduates. We have a very exclusive clientele and only work with people with legitimate college degrees."

"And what about the free trial? How does that work?" I took another sip of wine, trying not to look at the beautiful set of legs in front of me.

"All you have to do is sign up for one of our memberships, and if you're not happy for any reason during the first month, we don't charge you. It's that simple."

"And I have access to everything?" I asked her.

"Absolutely everything. You'd be surprised how many people connect with someone during their first month and end up paying nothing."

"That must hurt your bottom line,"

"Not really. That doesn't happen for everybody, and the ones that do connect always refer us to their friends, so we end up getting the money back anyway. Do you have any other questions?"

"No, I think I'm OK."

"So, Phil, are you ready to get started? You really can't lose."

I didn't know whether it was the wine or Parker's legs, but I was ready to sign. And said, "Let's do it."

Parker gave me a contract with six pages of terms and conditions I didn't bother to read. She showed me where I needed to sign and when I gave her back the paperwork, I was ready to win.

When I got home that night, I had a bout of buyer's remorse and wondered whether I was making a smart move. I was excited by all the energy I saw at the agency, not to mention the beautiful women who worked there. If my dates were half as cute as the women working there, it would be worth double the money.

It took four days to load my profile into their computer and generate my top ten matches. At my first opportunity, I logged into their system and downloaded my list of matches and their email addresses. I read their biographies and sent an introductory message to two of them.

Two weeks later, I sent out seven additional introductory emails but only heard back from one woman. She lived in Brooklyn and worked in the medical field. We agreed to meet at the agency's monthly networking social.

The agency's social was held on the last Friday of the month in the Turkish restaurant on the ground floor of their building. Beer and wine were available, and 70s disco music blared from a pair of speakers hanging from the ceiling. I recognized Irina from her profile photo. She was shorter than I imagined, but her sandy brown hair and green eyes made her stand out. I walked over to her and asked,

"Are you Irina?"

"Yes. Are you Phil?" She looked at my shoes first and then quickly gave me an up and down glance.

"I'm glad you could make it. Meeting in person is so much better than just talking on the phone or chatting online. Can I get you something to drink?"

"I'll have whatever you're drinking," she replied.

I asked the waiter to bring us two glasses of Chardonnay. We touched glasses and drank to our new friendship.

"So, what do you do in your spare time?" I asked.

"I like everything," she replied. "I like dancing, music, and expensive restaurants."

"Then you and I should get along fine. We like doing the same things. Where are you from?"

She looked down at the floor, then raised her head and said, "I am from Russia."

"How long have you lived here?"

"Twenty-two years."

"What did you do before you came here?"

"I was a baby doctor."

"You went to medical school?"

"I went to a Russian school and could be a doctor here if I went to medical school."

"It must be tough not being able to practice what you studied."

"I'd rather be a clerk here than a doctor in Russia."

"I guess we take a lot for granted."

Bill Clinton was running again in 1996, and I was curious what Irina thought. "What do you think about the presidential election?"

"I'm for Perot," she replied.

"Why? He doesn't have a chance of winning."

"He's rich and knows how to make money. He should be able to run a government."

I didn't quite get her logic. If I were to listen to her, we could have crack dealers running the country. They're rich and know how to run their gangs. "So, are you an independent, or do you vote Republican?"

"I'm a Republican. I don't like Clinton because he cheats on his wife and is the worst President in U.S. history."

"Actually, if you look at the facts, he's one of the best Presidents we've ever had. He had the lowest unemployment in thirty years, created 22 million new jobs, brought the crime rate to its lowest level in two decades, and converted the largest budget deficit into a surplus. Very few Presidents can claim that level of success."

"But what about GDP?" she asked.

After this conversation, I was sure she couldn't spell GDP, much less explain what it meant, but I didn't think a discussion of macroeconomics was appropriate at the time.

Two and a half hours later, we were the last ones in the restaurant. We left together, agreed to meet again, and then went our separate ways. Irina took the F Train to Brighton Beach while I took a cab to the Upper West Side.

Irina and I met a couple more times over the next few weeks. I made a point of changing our meeting locations to keep things interesting, and she liked each place better than the last. Though we were on opposite sides of the political fence, she had a charm and beauty that kept me eerily attracted to her. We were having drinks one night when she said we needed to have a talk. Any time someone tells you they need to have a talk with you, it usually isn't good.

"Phil," she said, "I need to tell you something."

I picked up my beer and took a sip. I knew she couldn't be pregnant, so that was one thing I didn't have to worry about.

"I told my husband about our friendship, and it made him very upset."

I picked up my glass, but this time I took more of a gulp than a sip. "You never told me you were married."

She sheepishly looked up at me and said, "I wanted to tell you, but I never got the chance."

Maybe she wasn't as dumb as I thought. "We've been out over seven times now. You could have blurted it out in between drinks or trips to the ladies' room."

"I didn't want that to get in the way of us becoming friends. Anyway, my husband doesn't live with me. He lives in his art studio and just comes home when he needs something."

It wasn't hard figuring out what kind of artist her husband was. A bullshit artist. I didn't have a problem with her being married. It was a bit of a turn on, but I would have rather known sooner than later. If she had hidden that about herself, what else could she be hiding?

Irina and I kept dating after she told me about her husband, but we never spent the night together. She maintained her fidelity to her absentee husband by only engaging in oral or manual sex. She considered anything more to be cheating. As long as I got some satisfaction, I wasn't arguing.

Two weeks later I got a call from Irina while I was sitting at work.

"Phil. We have to stop seeing each other."

"Is there a problem?"

"I still love my husband and if I keep seeing you, he might never come back."

"You might love him," I told her. "But the real question is whether he feels the same way about you. If he loved you, he'd be living at home and not just paying you a visit every time his funds run low."

"It's my duty to help him." She said this with a true sense of obligation.

"Let me make sure I've got this straight. You don't feel comfortable with me, but you don't have a problem with your husband living with another woman. Good luck with that kind of love."

The next time I saw Irina, she was wearing a red hat that said, "Clinton Screws Anything." She had on matching red shoes and a grey blazer. Normally I didn't get bothered by political beliefs, but I was not going to sit with her wearing that ridiculous hat. I wouldn't want anyone to think I agreed with her.

I looked at her and said, "You have to take that hat off."

"Why? It matches my shoes."

"Because I don't think wearing a hat that disparages the President is right."

"It's Hillary's fault. If she kept him happy, he wouldn't be chasing after kids."

"First of all, his relationship with the intern was between consenting adults. Plus, you don't know what arrangement he may have had with Hillary." I looked her in the face and continued. "All that's beside the point. Your hat offends me, and I'm asking you to take it off."

"I'm not taking it off. I have freedom of speech and a right to wear this."

"You're right. You do have a right to wear anything you want, but I have a right not to be seen with people who wear dumb hats."

She was giving me the perfect excuse to end our relationship, and I took advantage of the opportunity. I got up and walked away, laughing. She condemned Bill Clinton for doing the same thing she let her husband do, which sounded like textbook hypocrisy.

When I look back at the past few months. This was my first internet dating experience, and I wasn't quite sure how to judge it. When I first met Irina, I thought I had found a treasure, but after being with her for a few months, I realized my treasure chest was filled with Fool's Gold.

Jogging into the Past

When I heard that our annual sales meeting would be held in Dry Gulch, Arizona, I couldn't wait to get on the plane. The weather would be a skin soothing 75 degrees instead of the 25 it was in New York, and there would be clear blue skies instead of the grey overcast ones I saw out my office window. Magnificent mountains surrounded the city, while citrus trees with real oranges and lemons could be seen on people's lawns. There were a lot of things to like about Arizona, but then again, how could you have fun at a sales meeting in a town where the bars closed at 1:00 AM.? In order to do any serious bar hopping, you had to start in the middle of the afternoon,

Dry Gulch was a wealthy suburb of Phoenix with a population of just under 100,000. A beautiful city where baseball teams held their spring training, professional golf tournaments were held every year, and the city government was lobbying to sponsor a major tennis event.

The population of Dry Gulch was like Ivory soap, 99% white. The only black people I saw were working in Walmart. The Spanish-speaking people were gardeners, and the Native Americans seldom ventured off the reservation.

I was the "Salesperson of the Year" for the second straight year and was asked to deliver the keynote address at the awards banquet. It was to be a speech about what made me successful. And it was rumored that I would be offered the new Regional Sales Manager's position. I was the only black person at my company, and after seven years, I was looking forward to good things happening.

We were staying at the Dry Gulch Plaza, a sprawling complex with people catering to our every desire. You could play tennis on a professional court, take a swim in an Olympic-sized swimming pool, or visit the health club and get a free massage. One of the premier restaurants in Arizona sat in the middle of this sprawling complex. I checked into my room to put a little more polish on my speech for the award banquet. I thought a nice jog would be the perfect way to relax before the evening. I changed into my running clothes, did some stretches, and asked the concierge where I could run. She drew a map of a trail that would take me through one of the nicest neighborhoods in the area. I thanked her, stuck the map in my shorts, and started running along the course.

Starting on Dry Gulch Road and turning right on Mockingbird Lane, I followed the path and then turned on Bubble Head Drive. The homes in this neighborhood had breathtaking views of the mountains. Very few were multilevel, with many sitting behind gates or walls. Some of the homes had carports on the side or circular driveways in front. One of the carports housed a Lamborghini and two Ferraris. The same artificial turf I had seen at the hotel surrounded every house in this neighborhood. My lungs loved the clean air, and I was having as much fun looking at the homes as running. As I ran down Bubble Head Drive, a car started following me. I let it pass and kept running, occasionally wiping the sweat from my brow. The car then slowed down and waited for me. I still paid no attention and ran past it again. After I went another two blocks, the car resumed following me.

The car finally pulled up alongside me, and a man sitting inside rolled down the window and asked. "Excuse me, can I ask what you're doing?

"I'm just out for a little jog."

"This is a private neighborhood."

"I thought I was in Dry Gulch."

"You are."

"This is where I was told to run."

"We've had some robberies in the area, and we got a call from some people who saw you casing the neighborhood."

"All I was doing was jogging and looking at the architecture of some of the homes."

"Are you an architect?" he asked.

"I don't think that matters,"

"Well, if you're just running, why were you going over the same blocks?"

"I was lost."

"Do you have any identification?"

"I didn't carry my wallet because I didn't think I'd need it."

"Are you staying around here?"

"I'm staying at the Dry Gulch Plaza. They told me they tell all their guests to run here."

"Do you have any proof you're staying there, like a hotel key or something?"

"If I didn't have a pocket for my wallet, where do you think I was gonna put the key?"

"If you can't show us something, then you're going to have to be escorted out of the neighborhood."

"Wait a minute. I have a map the concierge gave me. That should prove where I got it."

"You could have gotten that map at any tourist office. That proves nothing."

"I'm not getting in your car and going anywhere!"

"If you can't show us any identification, or proof that you're staying in a hotel near here, we're going to have to hold you for the police."

A Dry Gulch Police car arrived ten minutes later to back up the two security guards. I was mad and wasn't going to be escorted to my hotel in a police car when I hadn't done anything.

"What's the problem?" the officer asked.

"We got a call that this man was wandering through the neighborhood checking out some of the houses. He has no ID and can't prove he's staying in the area. We offered to give him a ride, but he refused, so we decided to get you involved."

"Thanks for calling. They've had a lot of problems in Phoenix with these jogger purse snatchings. I hope these guys aren't trying to branch out."

"I've never been here before, and I don't know anything about any local crime waves. I was just out jogging and told these guys where I was staying. I even showed them the map I got from the concierge." The officer listened but wasn't taking my word.

"The way I see it, you got two choices. I can either take you to the hotel you say you're staying at, or I can take you downtown to the station?"

"You want to take me to the station when I didn't do anything? I was minding my own business and these guys started harassing me and now you want to take me to jail?"

"If you don't tell me where you want to go by the time you get in the back seat of my car, you will be spending the night in jail. Now, which one is it?"

"Like I said, I'm staying at the Dry Gulch Plaza."

I got in the police car and was taken back to my hotel. While the police were taking me back to the hotel, they watched someone speed through a red light and did nothing. I was supposed to be speaking in an hour and was missing the cocktail reception. That was the only reason I told the officer to take me back to the hotel. We walked through the lobby and saw our CEO talking to the Vice President of Sales. They saw me being escorted by the police, walked over, and started talking to the police officers.

"Is there a problem here?"

"We're trying to check this guy out. He said he's staying here, and we've had a lot of robberies in the area."

"I don't think he's your man."

"Do you know him?"

"Yes, he works for us."

"Then we'll release him on your word. Thank you and enjoy the rest of your stay in Arizona."

I ran back to my room, quickly changed clothes without taking a shower or brushing my teeth, and ran back to the main ballroom to deliver my speech. Unfortunately, the speech did not come off as well as I had wanted, and the punch lines packed very little wallop. That next evening, I was told they offered the job to Jim Leblanc. I headed to the airport, realizing my career was being put on a treadmill because I got caught jogging into the past.

The Loser's Line

My plane had just landed, and I was so tired I could have fallen asleep waiting in line for my bags. The flight from Amsterdam was turbulence friendly, and I had a hard time getting any sleep. Waiting for things was one of the pet peeves I developed after moving to New York. As a matter of fact, I didn't like standing in lines or waiting for anything. A woman waiting for her bags, whom I had seen on the plane, walked towards me, looking for her bags. We briefly caught eyes and spoke.

"What did you think about that flight?"

"There were a couple of times when I had to say a silent prayer, out loud," she laughed.

"I don't know what's worse, going through turbulence or waiting for these bags. My name's Miles." I stuck my hand out, she grabbed it, and smiled.

"My name's Caroline," she said, continuing to shake my hand.

"How long were you in Amsterdam?"

"A week," she replied. "I was there for an audition. What about you?"

"I started in France, traveled through Belgium, and spent the last three days in Amsterdam."

"Sounds like a lot of fun," she said.

"It was fun, but I'm glad to be home. Now all we have to do is wait for these bags."

"After that, we're going to wait on another line to get a cab," she joked.

"I have a car picking me up. Where are you going?"

"I live on the Upper West Side."

"If you want, I'm going that way and can drop you off."

"Are you sure?" she asked. "I wouldn't want to take you out of your way."

"I'm going to 83rd and Columbus, so it's no big deal."

Ten minutes later, the bags started coming down the carousel. We grabbed them and headed towards Customs with our passports in hand. It was just one more line we had to suffer through before finally heading home. After passing through Customs, we walked to Ground Transportation where I saw a guy holding a sign with my name on it. I signaled him, and he pointed us to a black town car. Though I was glad to be going home, I wasn't happy to be stuck in traffic on the Van Wyck. It was bumper to bumper and just another line holding me up. The only good thing about the awful traffic was that it gave Caroline and me a chance to get acquainted. When we got to her place, we traded numbers and agreed to meet again.

The driver dropped me off and I walked up the stairs to my apartment. I opened the door, took my shoes off, and sunk into the couch. I put my head back and thought about the work I had in front of me. I was about to invest every penny I had, and some I didn't, into a celebrity themed nightclub. Every nickel I had saved, and some I was borrowing, was being sunk into this club.

I got up the next morning with a clear understanding of what I needed to do. The worst part about taking a vacation is getting back. The first thing on my list was to walk to the bank and sign papers for a business loan.

I walked into the bank and went up to the woman at the Information Desk. "My name's Miles Stuart, and I'm here to sign some papers for a business loan."

"Ok. Mr. Stuart," she replied. "If you could wait over there on our commercial business line, someone will see you shortly." She pointed to a line on the other side of the lobby.

I walked over and was the third person on the line. While I stood there, I tried to figure out how long it would be before I got to see someone. My guess was twenty minutes. I looked at my watch and figured it might be closer to forty minutes before I would get out of there. While I waited on the line, a guy walked over to me and asked me for the time.

"It's 10:15." Though there was no chance of rain, he wore a long trench coat with the middle three buttons fastened and looked around the bank with a nervous twitch in his right hand.

"Is this the line for people looking to take out money?" he asked.

"I guess you could say that."

The man turned and nodded his head, and then he and an associate yelled out that it was a holdup and nobody better move. He unbuttoned his coat and pulled out a sawed-off shotgun, and pointed it in the air.

"I don't want to use this, but if I do, some of you won't be going home tonight." His accomplice went from one teller to the next, having them empty their drawers of all the paper money.

I was too scared to do anything and watched the robbery, which took less than five minutes. They were in and out of the bank faster than a politician at a truth conference. The only thing I could think of was leaving. I headed towards the door but was told by a security guard that everyone would have to stay and talk to the police. This was never part of what I had planned for my day.

The police arrived ten minutes after the burglars left and told everyone they had to be interviewed before being allowed to leave. As much as I wanted to get out of there, I knew how important it was to help the police catch those guys. I waited for a detective to speak to me, but noticed on two separate occasions people talking to the police, followed by quick glances in my direction.

One of the detectives finally walked up to me and took me to one of the small offices in the back of the bank.

"Sir," he asked. "Can you tell me what you saw?"

"I don't know," I replied. "It all happened so fast."

"It would help us if you could come down to the station and answer a few questions."

"I have a meeting I need to be at," I told him.

"Well, it shouldn't take too long. We'll get you out as soon as we can," he assured me.

I agreed to go and rode in the back of the detective's car. Of all the people in the bank when the robbery occurred, I was the only one going to the station, and didn't think my eyes were any better than anyone else's. We got to the station, and I was ushered into an interview room.

"Mr. Stuart, we know you were in the bank when the robbery occurred and wanted to ask you a few questions."

"Sure. But like I told the other detective, everything happened so fast I didn't see much."

"That's OK. Take your time," he replied. "I just want you to know that we appreciate you coming down here. You don't have to say anything that can be used in court. Plus, if any of this legal stuff sounds too complicated, we can always get you a lawyer to explain it. Does that sound OK?"

"I guess so, but I don't know why I'd need a lawyer."

"I know," said the detective, "But the law says I have to tell you about all the services we offer. It's really no big deal."

The detective, sporting a crew cut on top and a potbelly in the middle, asked me about everything but the size of my shoes. He then excused himself from the room. I wondered if I was free to go but waited for him to come back.

Ten minutes later another officer came in, introduced himself, sat down, and continued the questioning. He was much younger than the previous officer, without the same even temperament.

"Let's cut to the chase Stuart," He pounded a pad on the table and said, "I want to know about your friends in the bank."

"What are you talking about? I never saw those guys before, and I was as terrified as everyone else." I kept my hands in my lap, trying not to get excited.

"You were seen talking to one of them right before the robbery. I'm giving you a chance to help yourself. Who were they?"

"I'm telling you, I never saw those guys before. I was there for a business loan."

"Is that what you're calling it these days? Several witnesses saw you speaking to them before they pulled off the heist. What were you talking about?"

"He asked me for the time and whether the line I was on was for withdrawing money."

"Then you admit you talked to him about taking money."

"Not the way you're trying to put it."

"Then what way do you put it?" he asked. "Where were you meeting to split the money?" At this point, he was shouting, with spit occasionally coming out of his mouth.

After two hours of questioning, they finally let me go. I hadn't been home twenty-four hours, and I was being questioned for robbing a bank I did business with. I'd have to be dumber than stupid to do that and think I was going to get away.

I was still shaken hours after I had left the police station. Bad enough that I could have been hurt in the robbery, but to be accused of being part of the gang was hard to swallow. I missed lunch, went home, and headed straight to the liquor cabinet. Two glasses of Grand Marnier later, I was able to laugh at the absurdity of it all.

Two days later I called Caroline to see if she wanted to get together, and we agreed to meet for drinks that Friday evening.

When I met Caroline at Danny's Irish Pub, she looked even better than when we met. She wore a brown leather skirt, a white silk blouse, and a pearl necklace. She smiled warmly, hugged me and kissed me on the side of my face.

"I've got some good news," she said. "I'm going to be playing with the Dutch Symphony Orchestra." She could hardly sit still.

"Well, that calls for a celebration," I responded. I summoned the waiter and ordered a bottle of Moet.

"I have to be back in Amsterdam in two weeks."

"For how long?" I was happy for her, but sorry I wouldn't get a chance to develop our relationship before she hit the road.

"It's a twelve-month assignment traveling all over the world."

"That's wonderful. As much as I hate to see you go, hopefully you'll remember me when you get back."

"I'll be back before you realize I'm gone. Plus, you can always come and visit me overseas."

"Now that could be fun," I said, pouring her another glass of champagne and filling my glass as well.

We left Danny's and walked over to the club I was staking my future on. I never told Caroline I had an interest in the club. As far as she was concerned, we were just going to check out a new spot in town.

Nowhere was the club where I had a 37% stake and was the majority owner. Walking up to the main door, we tried to enter.

"Excuse me, are you on the guest list?" one of the bouncers asked.

"No, but I know the owners," I told them.

"Everybody says that. If you want to get in here, you'll have to wait on that line over there."

He pointed to a line of people who would probably never get in. Meanwhile, they were arbitrarily picking and choosing whoever they wanted to let in, and everyone else was told to wait on this line and stand away from the door. Anyone willing to spend what we were charging for drinks should have been let in before they changed their minds.

"Why don't you call your boss and tell him Miles Stuart is out front, and you don't want to let him in?"

"Look buddy, I told you if you want to get in, you have to wait over there. Now move away so these other people can get in." He looked annoyed but let other people in without asking them about the guest list.

I pulled my phone out and called Jeremy, one of my partners. He came out with two security guards and explained to the bouncers who I was. Both their faces turned whiter than sugar. Caroline and

I went inside and found a table on the mezzanine. I excused myself, went into the office, and summoned the two doormen for a talk.

"You guys are costing us more money than we pay you," I told them. "I don't think we can afford you."

The bouncer who gave me a hard time said," Look, I made a mistake, and I'm sorry for how I spoke to you. I didn't mean anything personal."

"But it is personal," I told him. "People come here to spend their money, and we're in the business of taking it. As long as they're not causing a problem, this club is going to have a first come first enter policy. So now I have two things for you to do. First, you're going to let those people standing on that line come in here as my guests, and then you're going to get your stuff and not come back. You like sending people to a line, so now I'm going to send you to one. The unemployment line." I got up, opened the door, and pointed them to the exit.

My Drug of Choice

My girlfriend's nagging had finally gotten me to face the truth. As much as I hated admitting it, I had a serious problem and needed to do something about it. I finished packing the things I would need for the next thirty days, to straighten out a problem that had gotten way out of control.

My girlfriend called the cab and hollered up at me, "The cab will be here in five minutes."

"I'm ready. We might as well get this over with."

Carrying my brown canvas bag down the stairs, I put it in the trunk of the cab. My girlfriend Phyllis climbed into the back seat of the black town car, and I sat next to her. She grabbed my hand, gave it a squeeze, and said, "I'm so proud of you. I know this is hard, but you will be so much better off taking control of your life."

I had no argument. She was right. I had let my drug of choice take over my life, and as long as I succumbed to its intoxicating power, I was lost. It was like I was in the middle of a jungle, with no clearly defined roads leading me back to civilization. Like many people who fell into unwise patterns of behavior, I got hooked early, and once I got started, shaking the habit was harder than anything I had ever done. Sometimes parental intervention worked, but when they weren't around, I went back to my old ways.

I was the only child in a lower middle class black family. My father worked as a mail sorter for the Post Office, and my mother worked in a small neighborhood department store. Back in the 1960s, these were considered good jobs for black people with no college education. Their dream was to provide that education for me, so I would have options in life not available to them. They made sure I didn't fall into any self-destructive habits, but sometimes peer pressure can be greater than parental influence.

When my friends in the neighborhood and at school kept talking about how much fun they were having, I turned on with them, and now, over three decades later, I was trying to get clean.

The cab pulled into the driveway of the Take Control Life Center and stopped in front of the main entrance. Phyllis and I got out of the cab, I grabbed my bags, and after taking a few deep breaths, we walked through the double glass doors.

"Are you checking in?" the receptionist asked. She picked up a sheet of paper and skimmed down the names. "What's your name, and who is your referring doctor?"

"My name is Tom Taylor, and I was referred by Dr. Frauden."

"Yes, I have you right here." She put a checkmark next to my name and looked back up at us. "You're scheduled to be with us for thirty days. Before I take you to your room, you have to talk to our admission counselor. After that, Ms. Taylor will have to leave, and you will start your road to recovery."

The facility looked an awful lot like a nursing home, but instead of elderly people riding in wheelchairs or supported with canes, I saw men and women my age and younger. Looking at some of them, I tried to guess what they were recovering from. Were they skin-popping heroin addicts or nasally challenged cocaine sniffers? Were they speed freaks who needed to slow down or alcoholics who needed to lose that bottle? There was probably every kind of substance abuser here, including me.

I was starting in the morning with a group therapy session where I would get up and openly discuss my problem. I felt a little uneasy about baring my weakness in front of a group of people I didn't know, but if that was the price of fixing my problem, I was gonna have to buy the ticket.

After talking to the admission counselor, I walked Phyllis out of the facility where a cab was waiting to take her home. We kissed goodbye, she wished me luck, and that would be the last time I would see or hear from her for the next thirty days. I walked back into the facility and was taken to my room. It was very Spartan. Along one wall was a single bed with a desk and on the opposite wall was a three-door maple dresser. The cream-colored walls were adorned with pictures of people who stayed in the room before me, with short testimonies under their pictures. I thought about what my picture would look like on one of those walls.

I didn't bother going to dinner that night. I felt a strange loneliness tearing away at my insides. I wasn't ready to meet anyone because I knew they'd be asking me questions I didn't want to answer. At that point, I wanted more than anything to turn on. Turn on and let my mind go like I had done hundreds of times before. I could sit back and temporarily forget about everything. Things like my boring job with little chance of advancement. I didn't care about my declining sexual urges or the extra pounds I needed to lose. Nothing mattered. I could shut the world out and look at life the way it could be, and not think about what it really was. Before Phyllis made me pack my bags to go to rehab, I was turning on from the time I got home from work until I went to bed. The hook was so deep, Phylis said rehab was my only way out, and because of our fifteen-year relationship, I had to listen to what she was saying.

The next morning, I cleaned up before going to breakfast. I found a small table in the back of the room, behind two women eating large bowls of cornflakes with sliced bananas and raisins. If I was lucky, they might be sleepwalking nymphomaniacs who might accidentally wander into my room. After a bowl of Captain Crunch with blueberries, I went to the group session being held in a small gym with about twenty-five people sitting in folding chairs in two concentric circles. Dr. Frauden led the session.

"Good morning, everyone. How are you feeling today?"

The crowd replied in unison. "Good morning Dr. Frauden. We feel great."

"That's wonderful. If you feel good, you'll act good. That's what we aim to do each and every day. We have a new member in the group, and I'd like him to come up and introduce himself."

I got up from my seat, walked to the middle of the circle, and said, "My name is Tom and I have been a substance abuser for the past thirty years. I finally realized how much it was interfering with my life, and I'm here to get help."

The group clapped and said in unison, "Welcome Tom, we're all here to help you."

It felt good having a group of people pushing for my success. "Thank you," I replied. "I appreciate your support."

I sat back down and listened to the rest of the meeting, which consisted of inspirational testimonials designed to make everybody feel good.

Later that evening, I was sitting in my room listening to the radio when I heard a knock on my door. I got up and opened the door.

"Tom, my name is Ralph Johnson, and I run the substance acquisition program."

"What's that?" I asked.

"Once a week you can order what you want, and we deliver it to you."

"What kind of substances are we talking about?"

"That depends on what you need. I have a menu for you." Ralph handed me a sheet that shocked me, given where I was. The prices on the sheet were considerably higher than what you would normally pay. Marijuana was $110 for a quarter ounce instead of the $80 most people paid. Cocaine was $110 a gram, ecstasy was $30 a pill, and anything else was negotiable.

"They let you do this here? I thought this was a rehab clinic."

"It is, but people can't be rehabilitated as long as they succumb to temptation. Plus, we only sell people things they aren't strung out on. If you have a cocaine problem, you can only buy ecstasy or weed."

"Doesn't that defeat the purpose of being here?"

"As far as the clinic is concerned, if people don't get rehabilitated, they'll keep coming back. It's all about money."

It was hard to believe the clinic was allowing this to go on, but if I wasn't seeing it with my own two eyes, I would have never believed the story. So I placed an order for a quarter ounce of weed.

"If you smoke in your room, make sure you put a towel under your door so the smell doesn't seep into the hall."

"OK. Thanks. This will make my stay a little more enjoyable."

"I'm glad to be of service. I'll have the stuff for you tomorrow. In case you need cash, there's an ATM in the basement."

"That works for me. It's not like I'm going anywhere."

Ralph wrote my order on a little pad and left to visit other customers. I changed the station on the radio before drifting off to sleep.

The next day, while I sat at breakfast, a woman walked over to my table and asked, "Do you mind if I sit here?"

"No, please sit," I told her.

"My name's Lisa," she said. "I think you're in the room next to me."

"I'm glad to meet you. How long have you been here?

"This is my fifth stay. I come back when I feel I need some positive reinforcement."

Ralph delivered my package the next evening. I rolled a joint before hiding the rest of the weed in my suitcase. I took a towel out of my bathroom and placed it under my door. I lit the joint and took a couple of hits. Before I could sit down, there was a loud knock at my door. I hoped Security didn't smell my weed, and I pondered not answering the door, but I walked over and asked, "Who is it?"

"It's me, Lisa. Did I catch you at a bad time?"

"No, I'm not busy," I replied. I opened the door and said, "Come on in."

She walked in and sat in the chair next to my bed. "It smells like you've met Ralph."

"Yes, I did make his acquaintance. Can I offer you something?"

"I wouldn't mind a couple of hits."

I picked up the joint and handed it to her. She took a couple of hits and passed it back. Then she moved closer to me, put her hand on my leg, and said, "Thanks for letting me hang out." She then kissed me and took the joint from my hand.

"I'm glad to have company."

After two more hits, Lisa pulled up her blouse, revealing her near perfect breasts, and pushed one in my direction. I licked her nipple and rolled on top of her. We made out for ten minutes before taking off our clothes and having pot induced sex.

Lisa knocked on my door every night for the next two weeks. Finally, one Saturday afternoon, she came by my room, and we smoked a little weed and had sex. Afterward, we held each other in a loving embrace, not saying anything.

"I have to tell you something," she said.

"What's up?"

"I'm leaving tomorrow."

"So soon?"

"My counselor says I'm ready to leave."

"And what do you think?"

"I'm not sure, but she knows what's best for me."

"Can I ask what you're in here for?"

"I have an overactive libido."

In the two weeks I had been hanging out with Lisa, I had no idea she was a nymphomaniac. I thought she dug me because I was good looking and willing to share my pot.

"You have to give me your number so we can stay in touch."

"I'd like that."

Lisa crawled out from under the covers and put her clothes back on. I felt a little guilty. She was trying to get control of her overactive libido, and I was unintentionally keeping her going in the wrong direction.

My thirty days had finally passed, and I was having my exit interview before being released to go home.

"Tom," my counselor asked, "What have you learned in your stay?"

"The most important thing I learned is that you must admit your problem before fixing it."

"You're absolutely right," she replied. "Is there anything you want to add to that?

"The second thing I learned was the importance of having a support network to help you."

"You're right again. That's what we try to provide. How will that help you with your problem?"

"For most of my life, I have been addicted to television. For the last thirty days I have not watched one program, and when I get home, I plan to give all my televisions away."

"Good luck to you." She smiled, reached out, and shook my hand.

The Golden Rule

I had just gotten off the plane and was heading to the rental car window. The flight was one of those rides that challenged my stomach's ability to hold food down. But, then again, what could you expect from a small plane landing at an airport built on top of a mountain?

This was the first time I had been back in West Virginia in over forty years. I picked up the rental car and started driving down the steep roads leading to the state's capital, Charleston. I had a business meeting scheduled for the next morning and wanted to spend the afternoon driving around to see how much might have changed. Charlestonians used to say they were too far north to be part of the South and too far south to be part of the North. That might have been the popular wisdom, but any place that had a high school named after Stonewall Jackson was on the wrong side of the cotton curtain.

When we moved to Charleston, the vestiges of segregation were still alive and kicking. Even though they had desegregated their schools three years earlier, people still swam in segregated pools, and all but a few neighborhoods were either all black or completely white. We lived in one of those integrated gray neighborhoods. Even though it was integrated, there were still a few people who didn't realize the civil war was over and their side had lost.

I once ran into my best friend, Davie, at the supermarket with his mother. I walked up to him and shook his hand.

"What are you doing here? I'm surprised to see you," he said.

"I have to pick up a couple of things for my mom."

"This is my mother," he said. He pointed to a woman standing beside a shopping cart. She was having a problem trying to get a box of noodles from the top shelf. I walked to the shelf and handed her the box of noodles.

"What do you think you're doing?" she asked.

"I was just trying to help."

"I didn't ask you to touch my food." She put the box back on the shelf and put another one in her cart.

"Danny lives around the corner from us. Can we give him a ride?"

His mother looked at me and asked, "How did you get here?"

"I walked."

"Then I guess you'll be going back the same way."

It was a testament to his character that we remained friends.

I followed the signs that directed me downtown, where I checked into my hotel and dropped off my bags. Things had changed so much that I barely recognized anything. Chrome and glass office towers replaced the three-story buildings I remember. Restaurants were selling more than corn dogs and watered-down beer, and women now held prominent positions in business. Charleston seemed to be moving into the present.

After lunch at a sushi restaurant, I got back into the car to revisit pieces of my past. Driving down Capitol Street, I noticed my high school had been transformed into a health club. When I got to my old neighborhood, I parked in front of the house we used to own. The big white stucco house looked as good as it did when we lived there. The other houses on the block looked much like I remember. The lawns were still well manicured and little black and white girls could be seen taking turns jumping rope. On the other side of the street, a couple of boys lobbed footballs to each other. Watching them play brought back warm memories.

We used to play touch football in the street and baseball-oriented games in a parking lot across the street from my friend Freddie's house. One of the baseball games we used to play was Home Run Derby. We had drawn chalk lines in the parking lot to designate what constituted a home run. One person would pitch, and everybody else would take turns at bat. Each batter got to hit twenty pitches and whoever had the most home runs was the winner.

Freddy was the neighborhood champion. No matter what I did, I could never beat him. I could beat anyone else in the neighborhood, but Freddie never lost. Not only did Freddie never lose, he also liked to talk trash while he was beating you. I remember the last time I played him.

"I don't know why you enjoy losing so much," Freddie said. He laughed and walked up to home plate.

"I didn't come here to lose. Nobody goes undefeated, and that includes you."

"I may eventually lose, but you won't be the one beating me."

"I wouldn't be too sure of that. It's only a matter of time until I get you."

"There ain't enough time in this century for you to beat me."

"Time has a way of running out, and your time is about due."

We flipped a coin to see who would go first. Freddie won the toss and chose to go first. He hit twelve home runs in his trip to the plate. I took the bat from him and hit two weak ground balls.

"I hope you can do better than that," Freddie chuckled. "I bet I could get my little sister to beat you."

I ignored Freddie's babble. He wanted me to think more about his barbs than my hitting. Of my next ten hits, seven were homers. I had eight hits left and needed six more homers to win. I hit five more and we ended up with a tie. That called for a sudden death swing off. After we both got one at bat, whoever hit the tie-breaking homer won.

Freddy walked back up to the plate and immediately hit a home run. I had to match him or else he would be the winner.

"You put up a good fight, but it won't be enough, because I feel a choke coming on."

"Do you know what Yogi Berra once said?" I asked him.

"No, what did he say?"

"He said the game wasn't over until it was over. I hate to tell you this, but you're counting unhatched chickens."

I stepped up to the plate and thought about all the times Freddie had beaten me. This was the closest I had ever come to winning, and I didn't want to waste the opportunity. I matched Freddie's homer with my own. Freddie hit the next pitch with the middle of his bat and the ball rolled into the outfield.

This was my chance to beat him. I hit the next pitch harder than I had ever hit a ball. The ball went flying out of the lot and across the street, breaking his mother's window.

Freddie walked over and shook my hand. "It looks like you finally beat me, but you still lost, because now you have to pay for my mother's window." Even though I had to pay for the window, beating Freddy was one of the proudest moments in my life."

Sitting in front of the house, I thought about some of the lessons I learned growing up. One of the things my mother used to talk about was the Golden Rule. Looking back at it, I realize there was more than one golden rule. The traditional one said you should always treat people like you wanted to be treated.

There were other golden rules I grew up with, and if I broke any of them, there wasn't enough gold on Earth to keep the belt off my butt. The rules were simple, but they were the law.

The first rule was the Golden Rule of Education. My parents would tell us, "If the teacher ever calls here to say anything other than you are doing a good job, you're going to be in serious trouble. And we're not listening to anything you have to say. The teacher's word is final."

The Golden Rule of Language said we couldn't use bad language in the house. The penalty for that was a mouth washing with Ivory soap. We also had to be home right after school and couldn't leave the house without permission.

One day, in a short bout of stupidity, I decided to wander away from the house and meet some friends at the playground around the corner. Though I was only two blocks from the house, I did not have permission to go. I played basketball for about an hour and a half before walking back home. When I got there, my mother was sitting on the porch waiting for me. I walked up the steps and said hello.

"Where have you been?" she asked.

"I was around the corner playing basketball."

"And who gave you permission to go?" she continued, with a stern look on her face.

At that point I knew I was in trouble. I tried to think of an answer that might be acceptable, but I knew none was forthcoming.

"I guess no one did," I sheepishly replied.

"Is that who you're listening to these days? No one."

I knew this was a trick question, and I had to come up with the right answer. "No, I listen to you and dad."

"Since I didn't give you permission, and your father didn't, I don't understand what you just told me. You said you listen to us, but you went off on your own. Does that make sense to you?"

My mother had a way of questioning you when you were wrong that made you understand exactly what you had done.

"Go to your room until I call you."

I knew exactly what that meant. It wasn't exactly death row, but it wasn't going to be a trip to Disneyland either. The only question was whether my mother would carry out my sentence or whether she'd outsource it to my father. I'd just as soon get it over with.

My mother called me down an hour later and sat me in a chair. "You know this is going to hurt me more than it hurts you," she said.

Based on all the rules of physics I understood, this was not physically possible. I was the one getting the whipping and was sure it was going to hurt me more. Maybe the belt would get worn a little thinner, but unless her wrist got tired, I was getting the worst of this deal. Unfortunately, this was not a discussion I could entertain with her at that time.

My mother told me to bring her the folding chair used for spankings. I brought the chair into the living room and sat it in the middle of the floor, waiting for the instruction to lie across the chair.

"Do you know why I'm doing this?" she asked.

"Yes," I replied. "I broke the rule and now I have to pay."

"You're right, but do you know why we have that rule?"

"I think so."

"Why do you think?"

"Because you're the parent and you make the rules."

"That's not exactly right. I need to know where you are in case I need to find you in an emergency. If I don't know where you are, I won't know where to look. That's why we have the rule."

I looked at the brown leather belt in her hand and knew it would be a short time before I would have to turn over and take my whipping like a man. I didn't know whether it was divine intervention, but for whatever reason, my mother didn't punish me, and that was when I went from being a child to being a responsible young adult.

Gator Done Got My Shoes

It had been over thirty years since I was last in this part of Mississippi. When I packed my bags and left, I had no intention of ever coming back. I got a call telling me my best friend from high school had passed, and I had no choice but to make that trip. Our friendship deserved that much. Though things had changed in most of the country, for me this was always going to be the land that time forgot. Time may have forgotten Blancville, but I didn't.

"I'd like to go to the Hilton." The cab driver nodded his head and turned on the meter.

"Where you from?"

"New York."

"You live in New York City? I hear you can live in one of them apartment buildings and not know who lives next door to you."

"I guess that depends on the building."

"I like the way we live down here. Everybody knows everybody's business."

As we headed downtown, there was nothing familiar about the roads or the people I saw. I tried to remember the faces of the people I had grown up with, but looking out the window, I recognized no one.

"What brings you to town?" The driver lit a cigarette and rolled down the window.

"A memorial service."

"The last guy to die around here was Mel Phillips. Was he your friend?"

"Yeah, we grew up together."

"He was one hell of a football player. They had a big funeral for him. The mayor and all these important people came. I heard they buried him in his jersey."

Mel was a great player, and some say he was one of the reasons they decided to integrate the local schools. The white high school got tired of losing to us every year. We took extraordinary pride in beating them because they had everything, and we only had our pride. They had the best facilities and the best equipment, but for us the field was the only place we could make it up, and our coaches had no problem running up the scores.

Just sitting in the back of a cab driven by a white man was different from when I had grown up. For most of Blancville's history, black people couldn't ride in white cabs. A company owned by Billy Paul Jones handled the needs of the black community. This was the town's version of separate but equal. When the white cab company went out of business, their operation was acquired by a company from a neighboring county, and they maintained the same policy of segregation. They eventually changed their policy after new federal laws were enforced. Black people could now ride in cabs, but there had to be a tarp covering the back seat, and we had to pay more than white people. I guess that was to cover the cost of the tarp.

We arrived at what used to be the Pickwick Hotel, now part of the Hilton chain. Just walking in the front door brought back memories I could have never imagined. Unless we were working in the kitchen or mopping floors, the inside of the Pickwick was seldom seen by the town's black population.

The hotel overlooked Stonewall Jackson Park, located in the center of town and one of the main recreation spaces in the city.

I relaxed in my room for a couple of hours before getting dressed and heading to the church where the memorial service was being held. I took a washcloth from the bathroom and wiped the dust off my alligator loafers, which fit my feet like a glove and gave off a shine I could see my face in. Though the church was a short distance on the other side of the park, it was only a five-dollar cab ride. I probably could have walked in less time than it took the driver to get me there. When I got to the church, I saw people I hadn't seen in thirty years, sitting with their families in the pews.

At the repast, I saw Buster Johnson, my second closest friend, growing up. Buster no longer looked like the slim athletic star of the basketball team, but looked more like the basketball itself.

Buster and I were on an undefeated team playing for the state championship. The team we played against acted like they were training to join the Klan, and good sportsmanship was not in their vocabulary. They cheated and the refs let them get away with it. The refs would call non-existent fouls on us and let them almost tackle us on the floor. I didn't know what they were getting paid or who they were getting paid from, but they were trying to deliver the championship to the white school. That strengthened our resolve to run faster, jump higher, and shoot with more accuracy. Though it was a close game, with seconds to go, Buster had the ball and dribbled past his defender. He put his finger in the air signifying the number one, closed his eyes, and shot the ball. He pointed at his defender and turned his back to the basket like he knew the ball was going in. The ball went straight through the net, without touching the rim, and we all screamed for joy. We were the state champs in spite of the refs.

"Hey Ricky," He grabbed me and put me in a bear hug. "How the hell you doin'?"

"I'm good. How's your family?"

"They're all doing good. Emma just had number five. You got any kids?"

"No, I can't handle the responsibility. I'm still out there trying to have fun."

"Where are you staying?"

"I'm over at the Hilton."

"The old Pickwick?"

"Yep, it seems funny."

"I remember when Black folks couldn't step in there without a mop in your hand. It shows you how much things are changing."

Things might have been changing in Blancville, but they never changed fast enough for me. I talked to half the people I had grown up with before leaving to go back to my hotel. I told Buster I was leaving and promised to give him a call before I went back to New York.

"You want a lift back to your hotel?"

"No, that's OK," I replied. "I want to walk through the park. I could use the exercise."

Buster looked at me like I was crazy. "Things haven't changed that much. The sun's going down, and you don't want to be in the park after dark."

"It's only a short walk."

"OK. But don't forget to call me before you leave." Buster gave me another hug, and I walked out of the church, heading for the park.

Growing up, we were not allowed to go into Stonewall Jackson Park after 3:00 in the fall and winter, and 5:30 in the late spring and summer. I remember one time when Mel and I were in the park five minutes after the curfew. It was the middle of July and we thought we would push the envelope a little. With big smiles on our fifteen-year-old faces, we walked down the path near the lake like we had every right to be there.

An older man with a cane looked at us like we were from another planet and said, "Do you boys know what time it is?"

"I looked at my watch and replied, "It's twenty minutes to six."

"That means it's ten minutes after you got no business being here."

"We're on our way home," Mel told him. "

"I don't give a damn where you're going. You shouldn't be here." He raised his cane and started muttering something we couldn't quite understand.

A small crowd started to gather, spitting at us and calling us names. They kept moving closer, and we had no idea what they were going to do. Mel told me to follow him as he bulldozed his way through the crowd. We ran like our lives depended on it, and truth be told, they did. We didn't stop until we were out of the park and on the block where we lived. It was a close call, but we made it. That was the last time I had been in that park.

I was exorcising the ghosts of the past by walking through that park. It had been thirty years since that incident, and I was sure I could get back to the hotel without any problems. I entered the park and walked along the abandoned road that ran through the center of the park and led straight to the hotel. The road was five hundred feet from the lake we used to visit, but were never allowed to swim in.

The afternoon heat had not yet dissipated but was not hot enough to make a leisurely stroll uncomfortable. People were gathered two hundred yards ahead to the right, shouting words I couldn't quite make out, but I did hear the words niggers and the Jews. That was my cue to disappear. If ever there was a place for a civil rights attorney from New York to be, this was not it. I walked to the other side of the trees and took the path that ran alongside the lake. If I was quiet, I could get out of the park and be back at the hotel in one piece, instead of being the uninvited guest of honor at an old-fashioned hate festival.

I breathed a sigh of relief once I passed the hate festival and figured I'd be back at the hotel in fifteen to twenty minutes. The sounds of the water running onto the shore were soothing, and in sharp contrast to the venom being spewed by the crowd at the hate festival. The honeysuckle on the left side of the path exuded a smell I seldom experienced in New York. I walked by a lamp post with 19th-century light fixtures and heard a big splash in the water. I thought about what Buster said about the park and wondered whether I should have taken that ride. I turned around and saw an alligator slowly climbing out of the lake and looking at my shoes. I stood there, too scared to move, and wondered what the gator was thinking. Was he thinking I might be wearing his sister on my feet, and maybe it was time for a little payback? I didn't know and wasn't going to stand around to find out, so I turned around and ran. I looked over my shoulder and saw the gator following me. He was moving slowly at first, but then he started picking up speed. I knew from watching movies that any time a gator chased you, you never ran in a straight line. You had to run a zigzag, and make sure you weren't zigging when you should be zagging. He was catching up, and it was just a matter of time before he got me, unless I came up with a quick solution. I saw a tree with a branch six feet off the ground and decided that was my way out. I grabbed the branch, climbed up a couple of levels, and prayed I wouldn't be there all night. The gator stood under the tree, waiting for me to come down. I couldn't shout for help because the people from the hate festival might come and help the gator.

As if things couldn't get worse, the gator started to climb the tree. Unless I could grow wings and fly, I was done. I didn't know what to do, so I took off one of my shoes, threw it, and hit him on the snout. I then jumped to the ground and ran faster than my legs could move. I had one shoe on and the other off and didn't have much time to think about what to do. I finally took the other shoe off and threw it at the gator, hoping it would make him retreat. I was tired, out of breath, and my legs ached, but at least they were still attached to my body and not part of that gator's dinner. I ran as far away from the lake as possible before seeing the road I had originally walked down. I followed that back to my hotel, walking barefoot through the front door and taking the elevator to my room to put on another pair of shoes. After catching my breath and thinking about what had just happened, I went to the bar, and after two shots of Southern Comfort, I finally cleared my head. Though that gator didn't get me, I did go home minus a new pair of alligator shoes.

Land of the Free

This was my first pre-Fourth of July Party. It was no different than a typical New Year's Eve party, with people eating and drinking and shooting off fireworks at the stroke of midnight. I had no idea that the events of that day would change my life in ways I could have never imagined.

My roommate's friend Shirley, and her husband Bob, had been hosting these parties for several years, but this was my first time attending. When we drove up to their home just outside of Phoenix, you could see the billowing smoke rising from their barbeque pit. The smell of roasted meat permeated the air, and an eclectic mix of hard rock was blasting from two stereo speakers perched in the window. A large American flag draped the front of their single-story adobe home, and their neatly manicured lawn was decorated with different cacti and wild desert flowers.

Shirley worked with my friends, Ivan and Jimmy, at a large real estate company in Phoenix. I was coming to the party as their guest and didn't quite know what to expect. I had been to many Fourth of July parties, but none of them ever started on July 3rd.

Jimmy worked in the mailroom at Kleptow Realty, while Ivan worked in the IT department, manning the help desk. They both loved their jobs and kept telling me I should consider working there after graduation. I had no idea what a degree in History would qualify me to do, but if the job market didn't improve, I might have to give that some consideration.

We walked down the driveway to the backyard, where at least two dozen people were eating, drinking, and talking about everything from sports to politics.

Shirley and Bob walked up and welcomed us to their home.

"C'mon in," Shirley said. She gave Jimmy and Ivan a hug and shook my hand.

"This is my friend Steven," Ivan said. "He's finishing his Masters degree at ASU."

"Steven, I'm in charge of recruitment and would love to talk to you about our intern program," she said. "Make sure you take my card before you leave."

"Thanks," I told her. "I'll do that."

"Why don't you guys go get yourself something to drink," Bob said. "The beer's over there in the cooler, and a batch of mojitos will be coming out the blender as we speak."

Bob looked about fifty and had gray hair with a touch of brown around the temples. His below-average height was in stark contrast to the large potbelly hanging over his belt. Shirley, who had blond hair with gray roots betraying her actual hair color, looked a little younger than Bob, but was in considerably better shape.

We passed on the mojitos, but did grab some beer out of the cooler. The food smelled so good it became our second stop before sitting at a long picnic table to join in the revelry. Before digging into the baked beans and grilled chicken, I introduced myself to everyone.

One of the men sitting at the table got up to make a toast. His short, cropped hair and long sideburns looked like they could use a trim, and he looked to be in the same unhealthy physical condition as Bob. He was sweating like a marathon runner and raised his beer can into the air. "Here's to the greatest country in the history of the world, and the forefathers that made it possible."

Almost everyone raised their drinks and shouted cheers. I refrained from joining in the toast. I had been born in Haiti and didn't think they were talking about my independence. Jimmy's relatives still lived on the reservation, and Ivan was in the country illegally from the old Soviet Union. He came over on a student visa and never left. I wasn't interested in starting an intelligent discussion here because chances were slim I would find one.

Though I tried to keep a low profile, I was called out by the fat guy making the toast. "Hey Steven, I didn't see your hand in the air. You got something against freedom?"

"No. I think freedom is a precious thing, but it should be precious for everybody,".

"What do you mean?" he asked.

"Nothing personal, but I try to stay away from political discussions at parties. They don't go well with the food."

Another guy sitting at the table jumped in. "You said you were a history major, right?"

"That's right,"

"Then, you ought to know why this holiday is so important. We owe our freedom to the founders of this nation."

As much as I tried to avoid a political discussion, I never failed to straighten out people either. "I hear what you're saying, but very few people were made free. Women weren't free. The indigenous people weren't free. The people brought over here from Africa weren't free, nor were the indentured servants. The only people who were free were white guys who owned property, and they weren't the majority of people in the country."

"Yeah, what you're saying might be true, but we're all free now, including all those people you named."

"I will drink to that," I said, and tilted my beer bottle in his direction. To get out of the discussion, I slowly walked over, filled my plate with more beans and chicken, and grabbed another beer.

For the rest of the evening, I confined my discussions to the Phoenix Suns, or the Arizona Diamondbacks. Sports always went along better with beer than politics.

After an incredible fireworks display, Jimmy, Ivan, and I thanked Bob and Shirley for their hospitality and got in the jeep to go home. We headed down Buckeye Road for the long drive to the apartment we all shared. We hadn't spent ten minutes in the jeep before I noticed a police car following us. I paid no attention to it until I saw the lights blinking and heard the siren blaring. Since we were the only ones on the road, it was obvious they were pulling us over. Two policemen got out of the car, walked over to the jeep, and asked Ivan for his license and registration. One of the officers walked back to their car to call for priors, while the other one started questioning us.

"Where you boys going?" he asked.

"We live over in Chandler, I replied. "We were at a Fourth of July party nearby."

"Have you all been drinking?" he asked.

"We had a couple of beers," Ivan replied. "That's about it."

The officer looked us over and asked, "Where were you boys born?"

Ivan lied and said he was born in Brooklyn. Jimmy said he was born on the Pima reservation, and then the police officer looked at me and said, "What about you?"

"I wasn't born here."

"Where were you born?" he asked.

"In Port au Prince," I replied.

"What part of Mexico is that?" he asked.

"It's not in Mexico. It's in Haiti."

"Are you a US citizen?"

"I guess so. My mother brought me here as a child, and I've been here ever since."

"Did your mother ever become a naturalized citizen?"

"I don't know. I never asked her. I always thought she was."

"You're going to have to come with me until we can straighten this out. Can you put your hands behind your back?"

I was handcuffed and put in the police car.

"What's going to happen?" I asked.

"You'll be held in detention until a judge decides whether you should be deported back to Haiti."

"By the way, where's your mother? We might want to talk to her."

"She passed away three years ago." It wasn't true, but I was not turning my mother in.

It was the 4th of July, and everybody I knew was celebrating freedom while I was being locked up to be potentially shipped to a country I barely lived in and didn't speak the language.

Dad's Surprise

The school year was over, and I was loading up my car to drive home for the summer. I had finally made the Dean's List and couldn't wait to tell my parents. For the past two years I had majored in the fun side of going to school, and doing well in class had never been one of my top priorities. I would be entering my senior year in September, and after all the hard work I did, I had a chance to get into a very good post-graduate program. My father helped me reach this new level of maturity. He, and the threat of his size fifteen boots.

When my grades arrived after my sophomore year, my dad took me into his home office and closed the door. Visits to his office with the door closed were never a good thing.

"Sit your stupid butt down," he said. "And I only plan to have this conversation once."

I could tell he was mad. My father was not a small man. Standing well over six feet tall and weighing at least two hundred seventy pounds, his hands were big enough to palm a basketball, or easily throw me across the room. But, instead of throwing me, he threw the grade report and said, "What the hell is this? I'm working my tail off to send you to school, and this is the best you can do!"

"I'm not saying it's the absolute best I can do, but I am trying."

"All I see you trying to do is smoke and drink yourself to the bottom of your class. That's not happening on my dime. So if I don't see some improvements, I'm going to make you two promises."

My dad was now standing. The look on his face, combined with his imposing figure, could have scared the devil back to hell. "What's that?"

"I promise I'm gonna stick my foot so far up your butt Lewis and Clark won't be able to find it. Then I'm going to yank you out of that school and make you go to work to pay for your own education. Now get the hell out of my office before I do something I'm going to regret."

It was at that point that I decided to take school more seriously. My grades this year reflected my boot-threatened attitude adjustment.

I finished loading my belongings and started the two hour drive to White Plains. My girlfriend Brenda was riding with me. She was always impeccably dressed, and everyone I knew was jealous of my good fortune.

Father's Day was coming, and I wanted to get my dad something special. He had just gotten a new Audi which gave me an idea. He loved that car more than anything, so I decided to buy him a set of deluxe chrome hubcaps. I called a few Audi dealers and asked about the different hubcaps available for his car. I looked them up, found one relatively close to our house, and phoned to see what they had.

"Hi, this is Benny. How can I help you?"

"I'm interested in a set of chrome hubcaps for an Audi A6."

"I can help you with that. What year is the car?"

"2013."

"That's a nice car. I drive one myself. What's your name?"

"Reggie Johnson."

"Reggie, are you looking to buy something today, or are you just shopping around?"

"I could do something today if the deal is right."

"Reggie, the deal will be right."

"I want a set of four chrome hubcaps. What do you have?"

"What kind of budget are we working with?"

"I didn't want to spend more than four hundred dollars."

"That's great. I've got a set of real beauties I can let you have for four hundred. They're normally six seventy-five."

"Does that include installation?"

"You didn't say you wanted us to install them. That would be extra."

"How much?"

"We charge seventy-two dollars an hour."

"And what about the anti-theft locks? Is that extra too?"

"If you're ready to do something right now, I might be able to get some of the installation fees waived."

"Benny, I told you I only had four hundred dollars to spend. Thanks for your time. I'll have to get back to you later."

If I was lucky, I'd never hear back from Benny. I called a few more dealerships in hopes of finding the right deal.

My dad owned an insurance agency and spent much of his time visiting business customers during the day and life insurance customers at night. He made a good living, but that didn't leave much time for fun. My mom decided to put her foot down and plan a trip for them to the Bahamas. They were going to lie on the beach, sample local cuisine, and try their luck in the casino.

When Brenda and I got to White Plains, I dropped her off and went home to unload my car. I opened the garage door and there it was. Sitting in the place of a 2007 Buick Regal was a 2013 Audi. It was navy blue with a gray leather interior and a Bose music system that sounded better than the stereo in my room. Driving this car was not a good idea because my dad was extremely possessive, and even more so about his new car.

I got a call the next day. "Hey Reggie, this is Bennie from the Audi dealer. I spoke to you yesterday about some hubcaps."

"That's right," I replied.

"We had an order cancel this morning, and I have a set of chrome covers I can give you a great deal on."

"What kind of deal are we talking about?" I asked.

"These hubcaps normally go for 139.95 each, but if you give me a credit card today, I can do them for four hundred, including the installation."

"What about the anti-theft locks?"

"We'll throw those in."

"And you can do all this tomorrow?"

"If you bring the car in early, I can get you out in about twenty-five minutes."

I thought about it for less than two seconds and told him, "You've got a deal. What if I bring it in at 10:00 AM?"

"That should be fine."

Under normal circumstances I wouldn't think about driving the car, but if I didn't take it in, I couldn't give him the surprise. The dealer was less than two miles away, so four extra miles on the car shouldn't be a big deal.

I picked up Brenda and drove over to the dealer. As soon as she got into the car, she was in love, and this time not with me. Compared to sitting in my car, this was like going from the Staten Island Ferry to the Queen Mary. It was only going to take thirty minutes to install everything, after which Brenda and I were going to go back to my room for some unconventional sex. We headed back to my house, and as I was making a left turn, a truck passing another car from the right came barreling through the intersection. Even though I was already in the intersection, the truck never stopped and hit the front of my dad's car, smashing the whole front end. The airbags deployed, and Brenda and I were lucky to escape without injury. The driver of the truck got out and started screaming about his right of way. After calling the police, who came and gave us both tickets, I called a tow truck to take the car back home. At this point, I knew my dad would be madder than words.

Brenda and I didn't have sex that afternoon because in less than twenty-four hours my mom, my dad, and his size fifteen shoes would be walking through the door.

I didn't get thirty-five minutes of sleep that night thinking of what my dad was going to do. I got up that next morning waiting for the cab to drop my parents off from the airport. A couple of hours later, I could hear the cab pulling into the driveway. My dad carried the luggage through the door and dropped the bags in the hallway. I gave my mom a hug and shook my dad's hand, wishing him a happy Father's Day, and figured I might as well give him the news.

"I've got some good news and some bad news. Which do you want first?"

"I'd hate the first news I heard to be bad," my mom said. "So, give me the good stuff."

"The good news is that I made the Dean's List this semester."

"Congratulations, son," my dad said. "We knew you could do

it." My dad patted me on the back. My heart started beating faster as I prepared to deliver the bad news.

"Dad, I took your new car to the dealer to have some hubcaps installed, and it was hit by a truck that demolished the whole front end."

My dad looked like he wanted to cry. I didn't know whether it was for the car he had just lost or the son he was going to beat within one inch of his life. Finally, he looked up at me and said, "Son, the most important thing is that you're all right. Being in the insurance business, nobody knows better than me that accidents happen. I can always get another car, but I can't get another son."

My father put his arms around me and gave me a hug, and this was the best gift a father could have given a son on what was supposed to be his day.

The Iceberg

I was rummaging through the shirt department at Bloomingdales when a woman walked up to me and asked, "Excuse me, are you Jerry Martin?"

I looked at her and smiled. "That depends on who's asking." She was cute enough for me to consider lying if I wasn't who she was looking for.

"I'm Jessica Walker. We went to high school together."

I stared at her face, trying to remember what it would have looked like two decades earlier. Instead of the long black hair I remember from high school, she had a short pageboy cut, and instead of the expensive designer clothes, she was dressed in a pair of black jeans and a blue golf shirt. She had the most unusual set of eyes that complemented her coffee-colored complexion. Though it had been nearly twenty years since I had last seen her, everything started coming back to me.

"You used to help me with my homework."

As I remember it, I actually used to do her homework. She was one of the most popular girls in school, and half the boys in school would have kissed her feet to be around her. Everybody was in love with her, and that was why I helped her.

Jessica lived in one of the biggest houses in Uniondale, and I never saw her ride the bus to school. She was always dropped off and picked up in a black Mercedes with tinted windows. Her father was a businessperson, but no one knew what he actually did. When she was old enough to drive, he bought her a red convertible that she parked in the back of the school, next to the teacher's lot. Under most circumstances she would never associate with someone like me. I was from a working-class family whose father struggled to keep food on the table. To help the family, I delivered newspapers in the morning before catching the bus to school. As soon as I got home, I did my homework, always reading a few chapters beyond what was assigned to keep me ahead of everyone. My mother drilled into my head the need to go to college, and win a scholarship to pay

The first time Jessica spoke to me was a week after our report cards had come out. She ran up to me after math class and asked, "How'd you like to make some money?"

I was shocked she spoke to me and surprised she wanted anything to do with me. "I can always use some extra money. What do you need me to do?"

"I'm having a problem with math," she replied. "You're one of the best students in class, and I could really use some help. The only way I'm going to get into a good school is if I improve my math scores in class and on the SAT."

I would have helped her for free, but if her father was going to pay me, that was even better. "When do you want to start?"

"I can't do it today, but we could start tomorrow. I can give you a ride after school and take you home when we're finished."

That next day, I met Jessica in the parking lot after school.

"I am so glad you can help me," she said. "My car is right over there." She pointed to a red BMW with a black convertible top sitting in the corner of the lot. We walked to her car, she put the top down, and we headed to the wealthy side of town.

"What schools are you applying to?" I asked her.

"Vassar, Sarah Lawrence, and Smith."

"You can't go wrong with any of those. Good luck," I told her. "If there's anything else I can do to help, let me know."

"That's why you're here."

Jessica pulled into the driveway of a Tudor house that looked twice as large as any other home on the block.

"Hi Jessie," said a well-dressed woman sitting on the couch. She looked like she could have been Jessica's mother.

"Hi mama."

"Who's your friend?" she asked.

"This is Jerry Martin. He's helping me with my math homework. We're going upstairs to my room to study."

"Pleasure to meet you," I said to Mrs. Walker. "You have a lovely home."

"Thank you, Jerry. I'll bring you kids a snack once you get settled."

Jessica's room looked more like a studio apartment than a bedroom. It contained a full bathroom and a king-sized bed with stuffed animals for pillows. She put a chair for me next to her desk and we did our math homework. I explained each of the answers, so she understood the logic behind the questions. When Jessica took her next math test, she got a 97% and did well for the rest of the semester.

Other than our tutoring sessions, when Jessica was around her friends, I didn't exist, even though I helped her raise her math scores high enough to get into Vassar. After high school I didn't see or hear from her, so I was surprised to see her twenty years later in the men's department at Bloomingdales.

Jessica gave me a hug and kissed me on the side of the cheek. "It's so good to see you. I often wondered what happened to you. I heard you went to Cornell. What are you doing now?"

"I'm working at Goldman Sachs. What about you?"

"I'm the Director of Human Resources for the Department of Social Services."

"Wow. That's the last place I would have expected you to be."

"When I got out of school I interned at Philip Morris. I stayed there for over ten years but jumped at the chance to run a department. Even if it is for the City."

"So, what was your major at Vassar?"

"Industrial Psychology. You know, I owe you a big apology."

"What for?"

"You were so sweet to help me in high school, and I treated you and a lot of other people very poorly."

"I didn't mind helping you. Plus, your father paid me."

"I acted like a spoiled rich girl and should have treated you better. I'd love to take you to lunch or drinks after work to catch up. It will be my treat."

"That sounds great."

"Here's my card. Give me a call, and we can go from there."

Jessica gave me another hug and left. I went back to shopping, buying a couple of shirts and a new tie before heading home to the Upper East Side.

Jessica and I agreed to meet at Fraunces Tavern that next week. I was excited about meeting her, but was wondering in the back of my mind what she wanted.

When I got to Fraunces Tavern, Jessica was seated in the back of the room, dressed in a short pleated skirt and a white blouse.

"How was your day?" she asked.

"Let's just say I'm glad it's over. And what about yours?"

"Working at the Department of Social Services presents new challenges every day. So what do you do at Goldman?"

"I'm an analyst for the Mergers and Acquisitions department."

"I always knew you were going to be successful. I'm happy for you."

Jessica ordered a white wine spritzer, and I got a dirty martini. We continued talking about what we had been doing since high school. Looking at her hand, I noticed she didn't have a wedding ring on her finger, so after the second martini, I commented.

"I always thought you'd be married to some rich guy with a couple of kids in private school. I never imagined you doing social work."

"I was married, but it didn't work out." She finished her spritzer and signaled the waiter to bring her another. "I was married for over ten years. My ex was a misery maker and not interested in anything I believed in."

"What did he do for a living?"

"He was an attorney for an insurance company, and his job was to make sure they paid out as few claims as possible. He got paid bonuses based on how much money he saved the company. Even though people had paid their premiums and counted on their policies to help them when they were in need, he did whatever he could to find ways to deny their claims."

"I guess some people will do anything for money. That must have been pretty hard to watch when you're working to help people."

"You're right. There was one case where the company didn't want to pay for a little girl's operation. She suffered from a rare kidney disease, and only two hospitals in the country could perform the procedure. He went to Court and argued the disease was congenital, so the company didn't have to pay."

"That sucks."

"They purposely stretched the case out for over three years. The family spent everything they had paying legal bills, and their daughter died. He went out and celebrated after his victory. That's when I told him either he had to change, or I was going to leave him."

"Did he make any changes?"

"Not only did he not change, he got worse, started drinking, and became physically abusive. I had to call the police on him several times."

"I could have never guessed you to be a person who would experience that. You had such a perfect life."

"It wasn't as perfect as you thought. I had a hard time growing up, and it had nothing to do with the clothes I wore or the car I drove. What if I told you I was abused as a child? Life is often like an iceberg. You only see what's above the water and don't see the 85% under the surface."

The waiter brought Jessica her spritzer, and I pointed to my empty glass for one more martini. She was so different from what I would have imagined. The girl who wore designer clothes and drove a red convertible in high school was now a sensitive person working for the City. She had become as beautiful inside as on the outside.

"And what about you?" she asked. "Are you married or seeing anybody?"

"Not really," I replied. "I've been married to my work. It's not what I want, but to get where I want to go, I have to make some sacrifices."

We finished our drinks, and I signaled the waiter to bring us our check. I reached into my pocket, grabbed my wallet, and took out my American ExpressCard.

Jessica looked at me and asked, "What are you doing? This is on me, so you can put that card back in your wallet."

"Ok. But you have to let me get the next one. This was fun."

After leaving the restaurant, we walked to the subway, and she took a train to the Westside while I headed home to the other side of Manhattan. We agreed to meet again the following week.

We met for lunch that next week and continued seeing each other every week after that. She gave me a good reason to cut back on my fourteen-hour workdays. There were too many fun things to do in the City, and now I had a partner to enjoy them with. Jessica and I were very different people when we were in high school, but two decades later, we were able to develop a relationship neither of us could have imagined.

Good Trouble

When my grandmother heard about the new voter ID laws here in Texas, she was so mad she could hardly get the words out of her mouth.

"I can't believe they're doing this. After everything we've gone through, they're trying to send us back in time."

"Why are they doing this?"

"They don't want Black people to vote. They know power comes from the ballot."

My grandmother had a way of explaining things that always got right to the point.

"Did I tell you what we had to go through when I tried to vote in North Carolina?"

She had told me the story several times, but I always gave her a chance to tell it again. It made her feel good and made me feel proud. My grandmother told me the story again.

"I'll never forget the first time I tried to vote. I walked into the poll station and was challenged as soon as I walked through the door."

"I'm sorry ma'am, but you can't vote here," the attendant told me.

"The Voter Registration Coalition says I can."

"I don't care what they told you. You can't vote here," the attendant said, with a scowl on her face.

"It's my right to vote as an American citizen."

"Have you passed your Voter Test?" she asked.

'What Voter Test?"

"There's a test for reading, writing, and arithmetic. You have to pass all three of them before you can vote."

I had just graduated from Howard University and didn't think I'd have a problem with any test they could give. "If that's what I have to do, then bring me your test."

The lady brought me a book with print so small, it was impossible to read. "The print here is too small," she told the attendant.

The attendant looked up and said, "Can you read this or not? That's all I want to know."

"No, I can't read that, and I bet you can't either."

"OK. You failed the test. Now you have to take our counting test." She walked into the other room and came back with a jar of jellybeans. "Can you tell me how many jellybeans are in this jar?"

"Do you know how many are in there?" I asked her.

"I don't need to know how many are in there. You do." She told me.

"Then how do you know if the answer I give you is right?" I knew any answer I gave was going to be wrong.

"What is your answer, and if you don't give me one, you'll fail this test too."

"We both know any number I give you is going to be wrong."

"You people act too smart for your own good. I'm going to give you the writing test."

She handed me a crumpled piece of paper and a pencil that needed sharpening, and then said, "Can you write down your name, address, and the church you go to?"

I wrote down the information requested except the name of my church. They didn't need it, so I didn't provide it.

"Ma'am, you failed two of our three tests and didn't complete the other one, so now I need you to stop holding up the line and causing trouble."

"I'm not holding up the line. If black people can wait three hundred years to vote, those folks can wait another three minutes."

"Ma'am, the police are on their way, and if you don't leave, you will be arrested."

"You want to have me arrested for trying to vote? If that's the case, I'll be proud to get locked up."

My grandmother loved telling me other stories about her involvement in the civil rights struggle. She talked about being at the March on Washington and listening to Dr. King talk about his dream. She told me about being on the Edmund Pettus Bridge and being attacked by the police for doing nothing more than marching to secure rights they should have already had. Now she felt we were being attacked again. But this time instead of using billy clubs and dogs that didn't know any better, they were using legislators who were dumber than the dogs.

My grandmother didn't look or act her age. She had a head of silver braided hair and liked wearing jeans and high-top sneakers.

"We can't let them get away with this. Too many people gave up their lives, and it's time for us to stand up and get into some good trouble."

"What do you think we should do?"

"We need to stop pussyfooting around. This is the same kind of bullshit they used to pull on us. I had to take tests administered by people who probably never finished high school."

My grandmother was the founder of a group called GAS. It stood for Grandmothers Against Suppression. Their objective was to bring attention to the new voter suppression laws. Those laws were making it harder for senior citizens, students, and people of color to vote. These were the people who had the nerve to put a black man in the White House. The people who claimed to love liberty were denying it to their fellow American citizens.

GAS had been meeting every other week for the past six months and was planning some sort of aggressive action. I had no idea what they were planning, but my grandmother said the world would soon find out.

We were having a mayoral election, and it was going to be the first test of the new law. Anyone without one of five types of identification would not be allowed to vote. Even though they could have been voting for the past fifty years, without the new IDs, they were effectively disenfranchised.

On Election Day, my grandmother asked me to drive her and two of her friends to the polls. When we got there, we were asked to produce one of the five required pieces of identification. My grandmother showed them her voter registration card like she had done for the past fifty years.

"I'm sorry ma'am," the clerk said. "I need to see one of these IDs." She pointed to a sign with the new requirements printed in bold red letters.

"I've been voting here for over fifty years, and this has been fine," my grandmother replied. "What's the problem?"

"We're trying to prevent voter fraud," the clerk replied.

"You haven't been letting us vote long enough to commit fraud.".

"We're trying to prevent it before it happens."

"Do you think somebody's gonna come in here, disguised as an eighty-three-year-old black woman, to try to cast a vote in my name?"

"Anything's possible," the clerk replied. "The governor is very serious about this."

"This is how stupid your rules are. If I have a license to carry a gun, that's OK for voting, but if I'm a doctoral candidate in Political Science at the University of Texas, I can't vote."

"I didn't make the rules," she said. "My job is to make sure they're followed."

My grandmother and her friends pulled out their cell phones and made some calls before sitting in the middle of the floor and saying if they couldn't vote no one would. Then she looked at me and said, "Junior, go get the camera out of the car and start documenting everything."

I ran out to the car and brought in my video camera. My grandmother made a few more calls, and in less than twenty minutes, about forty more grandmothers burst into the polling place and joined their silver-haired sisters in the middle of the floor.

"You ladies are going to have to leave," one of the poll workers told the grandmothers.

"Are you going to let us vote?" My grandmother responded.

"Only If you have the right identification," he replied.

"We'll leave when you follow the Constitution," my grandmother quipped. "I never read anything in the Constitution that says I have to have one of those IDs to vote."

The poll workers again asked them to leave, but they refused. The grannies called the local news to come and cover the protest.

People kept coming, and the protest got larger and larger. The polling attendants called the police, but the police had no idea how to handle the situation. With the local news there, they couldn't just beat up a bunch of old ladies. Maybe if they were all black, they might, but there were more white grannies than black ones, and some of the tech savvy grandmothers were streaming the incident on Facebook and asking their friends to come down and give their support. Two hours after my grandmother tried to cast her ballot, over three hundred people occupied and surrounded the polling place.

As word got out, students from the local university joined the protest, and then a counter-protest sprang up. A group of men who looked like retired Klansmen started waving confederate flags. Skinheads and a smattering of neo-Nazis, wearing Hitler mustaches and Gestapo helmets, complained that their rights were being violated. They told the police to get rid of those grandmothers or they would. Unconcealed pistols and automatic rifles were being carried in the open. The grandmothers were threatened with arrest if they weren't gone in thirty minutes.

Five more school buses of police officers pulled into the parking lot. At least forty officers, dressed in riot gear, got off the buses with the aim of stopping the demonstration. One of the officers pulled out a megaphone and said anyone who didn't clear the area was subject to arrest. No one moved and everyone joined hands, singing *We Shall Overcome*. Then the police made their move. They grabbed the black students, threw them on the ground, and put them in handcuffs. Two skinheads infiltrated the crowd and started throwing rocks at the police, prompting them to fire tear gas into the crowd, and in the confusion, beat anyone they could grab. Old, young, black, white, it didn't matter. Unless you were wearing blue, you were either beaten or put on the bus to be taken to the county jail. I went back inside the crowd and tried to find my grandmother. I found her still sitting on the floor.

"Grandma," I told her. "We've got to get out of here."

"Our work isn't finished," she said.

"You won't be able to do any work if you're in jail," I told her.

"It won't be the first time I went to jail, and if things don't change, it won't be the last. So why don't you take a seat and talk to some of these ladies? They have some interesting stories to tell, and you might learn something."

I sat down and interviewed one of the women sitting with my grandmother. She talked about being locked up in the Birmingham jail with Dr. King and said it was one of the proudest days of her life.

Before I could finish, the police started arresting the women sitting on the floor and grabbed my grandmother as their ringleader.

"Ma'am," the officer said. "You're being arrested for incitement to riot, disorderly conduct, and resisting arrest."

"Wait a minute," I jumped in. "How can you charge her with resisting arrest before you even tried to arrest her? She also couldn't be conducting herself in a disorderly manner if she was just sitting and talking with friends about the election."

"What are you, some kind of jailhouse lawyer?"

"No, but I have to look out for my grandmother's interests."

"Good, then you can look out for her interests behind bars." The officer confiscated my camera, put a pair of plastic handcuffs on my grandmother and me, and put us on one of the school buses headed to the police station.

As we were being driven away, we could see the news trucks from CBS, NBC, and ABC. They had all heard about the grannies and were broadcasting the story across the nation.

"Now the whole world knows about what we're trying to do. My good friend John Lewis would say we were getting ourselves into some good trouble."

I looked at my grandmother and smiled. "I never thought I'd be going to jail, but I'm honored to be sharing this ride with you." I gave her a kiss on the cheek and sat back to enjoy our ride to the local jail.

The Revolution

Gil Scott Heron would have been proud. The revolution was finally being televised. It wasn't being brought to us by Xerox, or making our teeth whiter, but across the globe, people were striking liberating blows for freedom. What was different about this revolution was that it was being broadcast to millions of viewers on television and across social media. The last time I took part in a revolution, it cost me five years of my life. My friend Marty and I were having a beer after work.

"What do you think about what's going on in Egypt?" he asked.

"People are tired of living 18th-century existences in the 21st century."

"I can't blame them," Marty said. "If I lived there, I would do the same thing."

"It's not so different here because we have many of the same problems. They're just on a different scale. That's why people are occupying Zuccotti Park. I'd like to go down there and see what's going on."

"They don't call it Zuccotti Park anymore. They renamed it Liberty Park and said they won't leave until the City meets their demands."

"What are they asking for?"

Marty picked up his beer and took a sip. "I'm not exactly sure. I haven't read anything that outlines any of their positions."

"That's why I want to go down there and see it with my own eyes."

I left work early the next day and jumped on the #2 train subway heading to Wall Street. Traveling to the occupation made me remember when I was involved in an occupation, in 1969, as a member of the Students for a Better Tomorrow.

The biggest issue we had besides the war in Viet Nam, was the arrest of students on campus for small amounts of soft drugs. We wanted ROTC off of our campus, and we wanted all Defense Department contracts canceled. In reality, the school had little authority to do any of these things, but we didn't care. I did not know then that our protests would change my life forever.

The train pulled into Park Place, I gathered my newspaper and made my way out of the subway. Though it was only 4:00, the street was filled with people hurrying towards the subway stations, heading to every borough but Staten Island. The Staten Islanders had to walk through Battery Park to get the ferry and take the thirty-minute boat ride to their borough. The ride was free, but that was the least the City could do for people willing to live so far away from the rest of New York.

Lower Manhattan was different from midtown. Instead of luxury Fifth Avenue stores where you hardly saw people spending money, lower Manhattan had smaller stores with signs in the windows offering large discounts to attract impulsive spenders. I saw more street vendors in five blocks downtown than I ever saw in Midtown. An energy existed that you never felt north of 34th Street.

I continued my trek down Broadway, finally reaching Zuccotti Park, now renamed Liberty Park. As I approached the park, the rhythmic beating of drums was getting louder and louder. This park's occupation was like nothing we had ever done in the sixties. This was as much a cultural occupation as a political one. A mini city sprung up with vendors providing food, free exercise classes, and political lectures from morning until whenever the day ended.

All ages, genders, races, and fashion types were represented in the park. Healthy discussions were taking place at tables sprinkled throughout the park. At the far end of the park, the drummers I had heard when I was walking down Broadway were getting ready to do another set. In the middle of the park, a woman spoke with a chorus echoing her words because sound equipment was not allowed in the park. Dozens of tents were neatly arranged on the south side, with generators brought in to keep everybody warm. It was a festive atmosphere organized to draw attention to the issues of income inequality and financial malfeasance from some of the biggest firms on Wall Street.

I walked around the park, listening to lively discussions and picking up literature outlining the protester's demands. One discussion had attracted a raucous crowd.

"Listen everybody," said a man wearing an army jacket and a coonskin hat. "It's time to let people know we're serious."

"And how are we supposed to do that?" an inquisitive man standing in the front of the crowd asked.

"I think we should block traffic during rush hour."

A woman, short in stature but large in message, walked to the center of the crowd.

"Brothers and sisters," she said, "we need to shut these mother-fuckers down. That's the only thing they respect. If we fuck with their money, they'll take their limp dicks out of our lives."

"And how do we shut them down?" a guy standing in the back asked. He was taller than anyone else in the crowd and wore rimless glasses.

"We need to shut down the exchange," she replied. "How much money do you think they'll lose if they can't trade for a day?"

Another guy in the crowd piped in, "She's right. They don't care if we sit here and complain. We're not costing them anything. They'll just get back in their limos and head home. But if we shut down the exchange, they won't be enjoying that ride."

Another woman, standing in front of the crowd, replied, "And what about the police? How do we deal with them?"

"That's why we have to do more than just occupy the exchange," the first woman replied. "We have to shut the motherfucker down."

The tall guy with the rimless glasses shouted back, "That's easy to say, but a lot harder to do."

"We're working on a plan. You just have to be ready when the time comes."

This discussion sounded eerily like one I had engaged in forty years earlier. A discussion between the Weathermen and the Students for a Better Tomorrow.

Dan Benton, the head of the Weathermen, was firing up the students at a rally on our campus. "It's time for us to take the gloves off," he said. "We have to let the establishment know we want change, and we want it now."

I was the Communications Director for the SBT and was at the meeting to provide a different perspective. "I agree with you," I told him. We should do something, but I'm not sure what we should do?"

"Chairman Mao said power comes from the barrel of a gun."
"That might work in China, but we're in no position to fight the police. We need to come up with a better idea than that."

"Until people started burning down neighborhoods, no one paid attention to people living in the inner city."

"Are you saying we should burn down the campus?"

"All I'm saying is nothing should be taken off the table. We have to keep all of our options open, but I like the way you think. We could use someone with your intellect."

"As long as we're not as bad as the people we criticize."

Six months later I left the SBT and joined The Weathermen, who decided the best way to facilitate social change was through the use of explosive devices. I disagreed with that strategy but was outvoted on important issues. We had a group responsible for acquiring bomb-making materials, another for building and assembling the bombs, and still another to place and detonate them. Their feeling was if the US could drop thousands of bombs on the Vietnamese, Americans should experience the same horror. Only then would they force their government to stop the war.

The leadership team thought this strategy was sound until two of the bombs accidentally detonated before they could be delivered. It killed two of my friends and the family that lived on the second floor of the house my friends lived in. I quit the group and renounced that level of violence. Even though I had renounced violence and had nothing to do with the bombing, the judge still sentenced me to five years in prison for being part of the conspiracy.

I thought my experiences were something people could benefit from and moved to the center of the crowd. I hoped it would at least make the aggressive fringe think about their potential actions.

"We have to be wary of quick fix solutions, like violence and unrealistic demands."

"What do you mean?" a man standing next to me asked.

"I'm not sure," I replied. "But we have to make sure we don't get involved in impulsive acts of violence."

"That might be the only way we can get their attention."

"My friend," I told him. "I spent five years in jail for conspiracy to bomb a building I didn't blow up, but five people died, and somebody had to pay. The Judge told us it made no sense killing people here in the name of stopping deaths in Southeast Asia."

A commotion erupted on the other end of the park, with people running in all directions. Hundreds of police entered the park and started beating and arresting as many people as they could get their hands on. I started moving toward Broadway when I heard one policeman point at me and scream, "Grab that asshole! He's one of the leaders." Not only was I not a leader, I was a follower trying to get out of the park. A woman running in front of me fell and almost got trampled. I bent over, helped her get up, and asked her if she was OK. Before she could answer, I felt a blow to the back of my head and went down to the ground. As I lay on the ground watching all hell break loose around me, I was kicked and beaten before I passed out. When I woke up, I was in the back of a police bus being taken to jail. A new generation was revolting against injustice, and I was being pulled back into another revolution.

Deuces Wild

It was as if I had pulled the trigger myself. My son was lying on what could very well be his deathbed, and I was partially responsible for putting him there. As much as I didn't want to admit it, I could have set a better example for him to follow.

I was the national spokesperson for the North American Gun Owners League, and my job was to speak on behalf of gun owners and their second amendment rights. I didn't care whether I spoke to a group of mothers protesting high murder rates or a local gun club looking to preserve their rights to own any kind of gun they wanted.

I was speaking at a local gun show when a group of protesters barged into the room to disrupt the show.

"You have blood on your hands," the leader of the group shouted. "You should be ashamed of yourself."

"I might have a little gunpowder under my fingernails, but I don't see any blood." I laughed and continued. "If anyone should be ashamed of themselves, it's you and your friends who hate the Constitution."

There must have been 25-30 people in the protest group representing a wide range of liberal constituencies. There were housewives, college students, grandmothers, and a few people who looked like they had just dropped in from the 60s. They were carrying signs and shouting slogans at the vendors.

"I'm sorry but you're trespassing at a private function," I told the group's leader.

"Was this advertised in the local paper?" someone asked.

"Yes," I replied.

"The ad said this was open to anyone 18 years and older, and we're all older than that."

"This is a gun show, and if you're not here to buy a gun or some ammunition, then I don't know why you're here."

"To stop you from selling them. Our community doesn't need any more guns on our streets."

"We have a constitutional right to buy and sell guns, and that includes the ammo to use with them."

"What about the rights of those thirteen school kids killed in that shooting last year? Didn't they have a right to go to school and not be gunned down? We need to talk about this, and we want to do it now."

"OK. I'll agree to talk to you. But we have to have some ground rules before I'm willing to go ahead."

"OK. What do you want?" the leader asked. She was tall with stringy brown hair tied back in a ponytail.

"We have to respect each other, so there should be no cursing or name calling."

"I can go along with that, and we think there should be no shouting, and one person speaking at a time," the group's leader replied.

"As long as the vendors can keep working while we talk, you've got a deal."

When we got in the other room, one of the 60s leftovers fired the first salvo. "I don't get it man," he said. "You're more concerned about us calling you a stupid motherfucker than you are about the kids who will die from those guns."

"First of all," I replied. "It's not the gun's fault. It's the people pulling the trigger."

"That's preposterous," one of the older women said. "If I ran you over with my car, are you saying the car didn't do it?"

"No, I'm saying you did."

Another gentleman raised his hand and spoke. "I think you're missing her point. If the person didn't have the gun, they couldn't do the killing."

"Look my friend, people were being killed long before we had guns, and they'll still be dying long after guns are gone. Our forefathers knew the importance of everybody having a gun. If we didn't have guns, we wouldn't have been able to kill enough Indians to make this the land of the free."

The college students jumped in, broke one of the ground rules, and started shouting, "Hell no, let's stop the show!" At first it was a quiet chant, but as more people joined in, the chant got louder and louder.

The protesters stormed out of the room, entered the main hall where the guns were being sold, and started turning over the literature tables and unplugging computers, preventing any transactions from taking place. The gun dealers started punching anyone who came near their tables. They didn't care whether it was an eighty-year-old woman or a high school student. Their rights to sell guns came first.

I called the police and told them there was a riot at the gun show and people were getting hurt. I've never seen the police get to the scene of a crime so fast. It seemed like they were there before I could get the phone back into my pocket. About a half dozen officers came carrying batons, ready to join the melee. One of the officers, who looked to be in charge, had a megaphone and shouted, "I want everybody to stop and take it easy. The next person I see throwing a punch or trying a kick is going to spend some time in jail.""

The police separated everyone into three groups. The gun dealers, the protesters, and the people looking to buy guns or ammunition. They made the protesters leave first. Then they let the shoppers go, but they let the gun dealers stay. With no one left to sell to, the dealers packed up their weapons and were out the door.

When the story of the riot hit the national news media, I was called into a meeting with the senior executives of NAGOL. They were sitting around the conference table in our Executive Briefing Room, and I had no idea what they wanted. I just hoped they weren't going to ask me to clean out my desk and turn in my keys. I walked in and exchanged pleasantries with everyone before taking a seat at the end of the table.

"Dan," the CEO started. "We wanted to talk to you about the publicity we've been getting after that gun show."

What I feared most was making my heart beat faster. The last thing I needed was to get fired. "Those protesters got out of hand," I replied. "And the old ladies were the worst. I saw one of them kick a guy in the balls." Everyone around the table laughed.

One of our Senior Vice Presidents then jumped in. "You know, they say all publicity is good publicity. Since that incident, our memberships have been up 245%. Contributions are coming in so fast you'd think we were printing money."

The CEO stood up and said, "Based on the publicity and contributions we've been receiving, we think you deserve a promotion. You are going to be our new Sr. Director of Corporate Communications. The job pays an annual $22,000 bonus, payable immediately, with an extra week of vacation."

It wasn't quite what I was expecting. I stood up and addressed everyone. "I'm honored and appreciate the opportunity to continue serving this great organization. Thank you."

For the rest of the afternoon, I thought about what I could do with the money. I could put it in the bank for Dan Junior to go to college. My wife needed a new car, or we could buy new living room furniture. I could use the money for any of those things, or I could buy something for myself. Since I was the one who earned the bonus, I thought about it and concluded Dan Junior wasn't currently enrolled in college, my wife's car still ran, and any new furniture could wait. I called Herman Curouge and told him I wanted to buy his Pederson Self-Loading sniper rifle. It was only $21,000 and would leave a little money in case Marie's car needed a repair.

I went by Herman's shop to get the gun. When I picked it up, it sent a warm sensation through my body. This gun was perfection. It was the prototype the Army used when they created the M-1, and now it was mine.

When I got home, I told Marie about the promotion but ,didn't say anything about the bonus. What she didn't know could never make her mad. I took the gun down to the basement where I kept the finest gun collection in our city. I owned seventeen handguns, including the six-shooter used to kill Jesse James and eight rifles, ranging from a Winchester Model 70 to a Barret M82. The way gun prices were going, it wouldn't be long before my guns would be worth more than my house. That was OK with me because I could always get another house.

Every Christmas, I treated the men in my neighborhood with a tour of my gun collection. I told the stories behind each of the guns, and the tour was so popular it became a rite of passage for the boys in the neighborhood. When they were old enough, they were allowed to come to my house and learn everything they could about guns.

That 4th of July we went to a picnic at Ken Forsythe's, who lived around the corner from our old house. Every year the Forsythes hosted a neighborhood party, with a spectacular fireworks display at the end of the evening. I saw a couple of people I didn't recognize and walked over and introduced myself.

"My name is Dan Sloman." I reached out to shake his hand. "Are you new to the neighborhood?"

"We moved here two months ago. My name's Norm Dunleavey." He grabbed my hand but gave it a weak shake. "So far we love it."

"We used to own a house two blocks from here. It's a great neighborhood," I told him. "What do you do for a living, Norm?"

"I'm an aide to Senator Brown."

I looked at Norm and said, "You mean the gun control lady?"

He looked at me and replied. "She just thinks we need to have a more balanced approach towards guns. 5% of the world's population should not own 40% of the guns. That doesn't make any sense."

"Thank God for the Constitution," I told him.

"My friend, times have changed," Norm said. "England's not coming back to recoup their colonies, and we get our food from the supermarket instead of hunting for it. Why do we need so many guns?"

"How about protecting our homes?" I retorted. "That could be everything we ever worked for."

"Unfortunately, the research doesn't support your claim. You have a better chance of staying alive if you don't pull out a gun."

"That's about the dumbest argument I ever heard. If a burglar comes walking into my house, he won't be leaving the same way."

"We're going to have to agree to disagree," Norm said. "I'm still glad to meet you." He slowly stuck his arm out and we shook hands once more before walking to opposite ends of the festivities.

Four beers and an hour of fireworks later, Marie and I got into her car to drive home. No more than six blocks from the party, Marie's car decided it wasn't finishing the trip. You could smell the oil burning from the engine and see steam oozing from under the hood. First a small amount, then what could be called a deluge. Stranded on the side of the road, with no other way to get home, we called a towing company and got them to haul the car back to our house. The good news was that we could get the car towed back to my driveway, but the bad news was it would cost me two hundred dollars to do it. After the driver put the car on the flatbed, we all squeezed into the front seat of his truck. The driver dropped me, Marie, and the car home.

"Honey," I said to Marie. "You've got to take better care of this car."

"I've been telling you for months that I needed a new car."

"You're right," I told her. "As soon as I get my tax return check, I'll see what I can do."

"You expect me to drive this?" She put her hands on her hips and pointed at me. "You spend our money building your own personal arsenal, and I can't get a new car?"

"I never said you couldn't get a new car. I'm just suggesting we get it when I have a little extra money."

We walked into the house, exhausted from the ordeal, and got ready to go to bed, when I walked into the kitchen and noticed the basement door was slightly ajar. The lights were on, and I remember locking the door and turning off those lights. I walked down the steps and saw the lock broken on my gun case. Two of my handguns were missing. My Titanium Gold Desert Eagle, and my Walther P99. I got a bad feeling at the bottom of my stomach. There was no sign of a break-in and I figured Dan Jr. had to be the culprit. I went upstairs and called his cell phone, but got no answer.

Marie came out of the bedroom and asked, "Do you think we should call the police?"

"I'm going to handle this myself. I think Junior stole those guns."

"How do you know it was him?"

"There's no sign of a break-in, so it had to be him."

"You make a living telling people to carry guns, and he's just doing what you tell people to do."

"The Constitution gives us a right to carry guns, not to steal them."

Marie threw her hands up and said, "He's our son, and he needs our help."

"What he needs is a swift kick in the ass and a couple of weeks in jail. That'll straighten him out."

"Maybe being in jail will make him worse. We can't give up on him."

"I'm giving up. When he gets back, I'm throwing his ass out on the street."

"We have to help him," Marie pleaded.

"Well, I hope he finds help because he's stolen his last thing from me."

I sat down at the kitchen table, trying to think about where Junior might have gone with my guns, and he could have gone anywhere. The guns cost me eleven thousand dollars, and I was sure he would try to pawn them or give them to his drug dealer for two hundred bucks worth of dope. Marie made a pot of coffee and sat down with me. Before I could finish my first cup, the doorbell rang. I got up from the table, walked to the front door, and saw two police officers standing on the porch. I twisted the lock and opened the door.

"Officers, can I help you with something?" The first thing I thought was that Marie may have called them before our discussion.

"We're looking for the parents of Daniel Sloman," one of the officers replied.

"I'm his father. What's this about?"

"Can we come in?" the officer asked.

"Why of course," I replied. "How can I help you?"

The officer looked down at the floor and then raised his head. "I have some bad news. Your son was involved in a shooting and is on life support at Bayside General Hospital."

My eyes opened as wide as they could, and a sense of sadness and then guilt ran through my body. "What happened?"

"He was at a known drug location, and a fight broke out. We don't have all the details right now, but we will keep you informed as the investigation goes on."

The officers got up and left, and I walked back into the kitchen with tears trickling down my face and said, "Honey, we have to go to the hospital because Junior needs our help."

The Mask

They hadn't cleaned the blood off the floor, and my stomach was still sick from what I had witnessed earlier. I never thought when I woke up that morning that I would be involved in a mass shooting. I was the Director of Security at The Big Deal supermarket in Liberty, Texas. I grew up in Liberty, and when we were kids, we used to make money by helping people carry their groceries to their cars. We'd accept whatever tips they were willing to give us. Sometimes it was a nickel or a dime, but every now and then we'd get a big tipper who would give us anything from fifty cents to a dollar.

We had three security guards in the department. One undercover, who walked around looking for shoplifters, one ex-football player who handled the tough stuff, and myself. Things were usually pretty quiet in the store. The worst things we had to deal with were people using stolen credit cards and the occasional shoplifter. Depending upon who they were, and their circumstances, we often tried to give people a break. I knew many of the people in the neighborhood and knew how tough times were. As affordable housing kept slowly disappearing, and job opportunities decreasing, our latest reports showed inventory shrinkage on the rise.

Two months after I had started at The Big Deal, a shoplifter was brought to my office, waiting to be turned over to the local police. She was caught leaving the store without paying for a basket of food.

"Ma'am," I told her. You're going to be turned over to the police."

"This is my first time doing this. Can you give me a break? I'm sorry for what I did."

"You were caught taking over a hundred dollars in food."

"I got laid off from my job, and my children haven't eaten since yesterday. I didn't know what else to do."

"I feel sorry for your family, but that doesn't give you the right to come here and steal."

"If I had the money, I would have paid, but I don't have it, and my family still needs to eat."

"Have you been in trouble with the law before?"

"No sir."

"I'm going to make you a deal. You take this food home and feed your family, but I don't want you coming back to this store until you can pay for what you take."

"Thank you. I promise you won't be seeing me until I'm working."

"And if we catch you stealing again, you will go to jail. Are we clear on that?"

"Yes sir."

We were losing two employees a month from the virus, our revenues had dropped 50%, and dozens of workers had lost their jobs. We were finally coming out of the worst part of the pandemic, and things were getting better, but still not looking good.

When the hospitalizations in Texas exceeded the available beds, a mandate was issued that required anyone leaving their home to wear a face covering. Initially, most people complied, but after a few months, the masks started coming off, even though the number of deaths kept going up. There was a belief that because people were getting vaccinated, it was time to go back to normal. I didn't understand the logic. The virus still wasn't under control. Countries that opened up too quickly had to shut back down after their case numbers started spiking. That we should get different results in Texas was developmentally challenged thinking. Premature openings didn't work in London, and they weren't going to work in Liberty either.

After the mandate was lifted, listening to the scientists was no longer a priority. The people who knew the least about the virus were saying the most, and too many people were listening. There was one city in Texas where the mayor told everyone to breathe on each other to prove the virus wasn't transmitted from droplets coming from the mouth. A group called the Free Face Society said wearing masks actually caused people to get sicker because when the virus couldn't escape back into the air.

The problem with the way the mask mandate was rescinded was that businesses had to determine their own policies towards mask wearing and be responsible for enforcing them. If they got in a pinch, they could call local law enforcement to come and arrest the people for trespass. With the mandate lifted, every store on the block could have a different policy, and the police had to determine which ones were important and which ones were not.

For the first time in several months, it was a good day for the company. Sales trends were moving in the right direction, and rumors were circulating that everyone who had lost their jobs because of the pandemic would be hired back. I was doing my rounds walking through the different departments, and initially didn't hear the commotion. I turned and walked closer to the shouting. Jasmine Hoang, the Store Manager, was talking to a guy not wearing the required face covering. Jasmine started working here fourteen years ago as an intern from the University of Texas and accepted a position here right after she graduated. Everyone thought she would eventually become our first female CEO.

"The Governor said I don't have to wear a mask."

"You're wrong. The Governor said each business makes their own rules, and our rules say you have to wear a mask."

"You ain't more important than the Governor, and If he says I don't have to wear it, I ain't wearin' it."

"Then I have to ask you to leave."

"You're kicking me out of here because I don't want to wear a mask?"

"I'm asking you to leave because our policy says you have to wear a mask to come into the store."

"I just came here to get a pack of cigarettes and a can of beer."

"You can't buy anything because you have to leave."

"I ain't leaving until I get what I came for."

"Then I'm going to call security."

At that point I walked over and introduced myself.

"My name's Julian Richards, and I'm the Director of Security. Is there a problem?"

The man, who wore a white tee shirt with the words *Liberate Your Face*, in red, said, "This lady won't let me buy my cigarettes."

Jasmine explained. I told him it was the store policy that anyone who comes into the store must wear a mask. "There's a big sign right by the front door."

"I didn't see the sign," the man replied.

"That doesn't change our policy. If you didn't see the sign, that's not our problem."

"You don't have to get smart," he told her. "Your people brought the disease here anyway."

"My people came from Vietnam, and the only thing they brought with them was the desire to work hard and share in the American dream."

"You can't share in the American dream 'cause you ain't American."

At that point I stepped in. "Sir, this conversation isn't getting us anywhere. We have a store policy, and we don't make exceptions. Let me make you a deal. I'll give you the pack of cigarettes, but you have to leave, and I don't want you coming back. If you leave now, I won't call the police. Do we have a deal?"

"Yes sir. You go a deal."

I gave him the pack of cigarettes and escorted him out of the store.

"This ain't right," he said. "The Governor said I don't have to wear a mask, and you're telling me I do."

"If we let everybody make their own laws, then we'd have no order, and we can't have that."

"I don't know who to listen to, you or the Governor."

"In this store you have to listen to me."

The man got into his truck and drove away, and I hoped that was the last time I would see him.

I walked back into the store and saw Jasmine. "You did a good job with that guy."

"I tried to explain the rules to him, but he didn't want to listen."

"I know. The State's really messed this up."

"And they want us to do their jobs. We shouldn't be put in that position."

"You're right. Starting next week, I'm going to have a security guard stationed at the door to deal with people who aren't wearing masks. You guys have enough stuff to deal with."

"That's great, because I'm tired of being the mask enforcer."

The rest of the afternoon went without any drama until the man we had asked to leave earlier came back. I never saw the gun he was carrying until it was in his hand. "Where's that gook bitch that threw me out of here?"

He spotted Jasmine standing behind the perfume counter and started shooting. He screamed, "You gook bitch! Let me see you put a mask on now. Where you're going, you won't need one."

People in the store started running in every direction, but towards the shooter. They hit the exits as fast as they could. Those that couldn't reach the exits kneeled behind counters or hid under tables. I took my gun out of my holster and waited until I had a clear shot at the gunman. Then I aimed for his head and pulled the trigger. The bullet hit him above his right eye, and he fell in a heap to the floor. Screaming could be heard throughout the store as people kept running for the exits, but the immediate threat was over.

The police finally arrived and walked around the store to assess the damage. Besides the shooter, Jasmine and four co-workers were dead. Three of the four were Asian-Americans, and we couldn't help but think they were targeted.

Things were starting to get back to normal a couple of months after the shooting. The security guard at the door was dealing with the mask issues, customers were coming back, and the employees were feeling a new sense of comfort. Things were quiet, but maybe a little too quiet. Paul, the security guard, had to take a day off and we were stuck without someone watching the door. An hour before closing, a man, not wearing a mask, came into the store and pulled out a gun. He pointed it in the air and shouted, "This is a robbery, and if you do what I say, no one will get hurt."

The robber went to each cashier and made them put the money in a dirty linen bag. He emptied eight registers before running out the door and disappearing down the street.

The next day, while I was straightening up my office and getting ready to go home, I got a call.

"This is Julian," I said.

"Julian, this is Hank, down at the police station. We got the guy that robbed the store yesterday."

"That was pretty fast. How'd you catch him?"

"We looked at the video footage from the store, and he was the only one not wearing a mask. After that, it was easy, and we picked him up late last night."

Q-Ball in the Side Pocket

It was one of those humid Tennessee nights, and I had just finished a ten-hour shift at the lumberyard. I was tired, and in need of a serious thirst quencher. I decided to take the fifteen-minute ride over to Billy Clyde's Roadhouse, which we all called Billy's. Opened over fifty years ago by Billy Clyde Washburn, it was now run by his son Cletus. Billy's didn't serve the kind of wine that needed a corkscrew, and the beer tasted awful. But on a hot day like this, I was just glad it was cold.

I parked at the end of a row of dusty pickup trucks and took a seat in the middle of the bar, in front of the television. On the back wall hung a confederate flag that stretched from the ceiling to the floor, and on the adjacent wall was a picture of a Tennessee regiment that fought in the Civil War. The wooden tables lacked tablecloths, and you had to ask for metal silverware if you didn't want to eat with a plastic spoon and fork. This was never going to be mistaken for an establishment of fine dining. Billy's was comfort food, and that's just what folks around here wanted.

I saw Earl Baker sitting with a beer, watching a baseball game. He used to work at the lumberyard but got fired for coming to work drunk too many times. Now he did odd jobs for anyone who would hire him. I wouldn't call Earl ugly, but his mug would never adorn the cover of any reputable magazine. His scruffy face possessed a permanent stubble of beard. Two teeth were missing from the left side of his mouth, and he had dirty blond hair with more dirt than blond. His left leg was slightly bowed, and he liked wearing heavy wool shirts regardless of the season.

"Hey Earl, how you doin'?" I asked.

"I could be doin' better, but I ain't complainin'. How's things over at the yard?"

"We been busy as hell. That big job for the County has been keepin' us so busy that nobody's got time to take a good piss."

I knew most of the people sitting at the bar except one guy wearing a red, white, and blue shirt with a big Q in the middle. He had a shaven head with about the same amount of stubble on his face as Earl. His black boots needed polish, and his jeans had holes at the knees. He was watching the game but obviously not enjoying it.

"Ain't this some bullshit," he said. "This is America's game, but I don't see no Americans playin'."

"You're right," Earl said to him. "People like us don't get to play real sports. Puerto Ricans took over baseball, colored people are dribbling the basketballs, and Canadians stole the hockey pucks. Us white people don't get to play nothing."

Earl pointed at the flag on the back wall and said, "There was a time when we used to do something about this stuff. Now, we got no rights in our own country."

"Nobody eliminated their problems better than my people. By the way, my name's Karl."

"I'm Earl." He shook Karl's hand and continued." We never had issues like this before. Anybody got out of line, we paid them a visit in the middle of the night and that usually fixed the problem."

"Yeah, but they're still here takin' our jobs." Karl looked around the bar and got nods from most of the people sitting there.

"My uncle said we would've hung more troublemakers if we didn't run out of trees." Earl let out a big laugh and took another sip of his beer.

Not to be outdone, Karl looked at Earl and said, "Compared to the Germans, those guys were amateurs."

"Are you makin' fun of my ancestors?"

"No, but people like you and me need to be thinking about what we can do now, instead of worrying about what people did a hundred years ago. Let me get you another beer."

"Thanks." Earl had never been one to turn down a free beer.

"Are you interested in doin' something about the way things are goin' in this country?"

"Yeah, I am," Earl said.

"I'm in this group that supports the President with strategic action."

"You guys talk to the President?"

"We work with his liaison, who tells us when to act."

"What kind of actions are we talking about?" Earl asked.

"Did you see what happened at the Capitol last month? That was us."

"That was you guys?"

"That's right. Our government was stolen, and we were gonna take it back."

"You guys are freedom fighters," Earl said.

"That's right. We had a plan to set up a new government and reinstate President Trump, but things didn't work out."

"What was the plan?"

"We were gonna catch Nancy Pelosi, AOC, and Bernie Sanders and put them on trial. Then, after we found them guilty, they were gonna be eliminated. President Trump could then declare martial law and call for a new election. And this time we'd be counting the votes."

"Sounds like you guys are doing something, and I like that."

"Then you should join us."

"Who are you guys?"

"We're called the Q-Brigade. We're patriots from all fifty states, ready to take back our country. We have a meeting next Saturday, if you're interested in seeing what we're all about."

"What do you do at the meetings?"

"We drink beer and talk about how the government sucks."

"Is it good beer?" Earl asked.

"It's free, and free beer always tastes good."

"Amen to that, brother."

"I can tell just by talking to you that you would fit right in with us. Let me get you another beer."

Two men dressed in suits, white shirts, and polished shoes walked into the bar and said something to Cletus. Cletus turned, pointed in my direction, and the two men walked towards me and Karl.

"We're looking for Karl Schtuler."

"That's me," Karl replied. "Who are you?"

"We're with the FBI," one of the agents said.

"What do you want with me?"

"We have a warrant for your arrest." the agent replied.

"I haven't done anything. What am I being arrested for?"

"We can discuss that back in our office," the agent replied.

"I ain't goin' nowhere unless you tell me the charges," Karl told them." I got rights."

The officer reached into his coat pocket and handed Karl a letter, which he opened and started reading.

"You're being charged with trespass, destruction of government property, assault on federal police officers, with more charges on the way," the other agent said.

"How can you charge me with trespass when the President invited us to go to the Capitol?"

"Unless you were a member of Congress, the Capitol was closed."

"How was I supposed to know that?"

"You could have asked someone."

"President Trump told us to stop the votes from being counted because the election was a phony scam. He's our Commander and we do what he says."

"I'm not here to debate with you. Put your hands behind your back, or this is going to get real ugly." He took a pair of handcuffs from under his jacket and placed them on Karl.

Earl stood there and said to Karl, "Thanks for the beer. By the way, where's that meeting going to be next week? I wouldn't want to miss the free beer."

The two agents escorted Karl out of the bar and into the back seat of their car before pulling out of the parking lot and taking him downtown to their office. After all the excitement was over, everybody went back to their drinks like nothing had ever happened.

A few months later, I saw Earl sitting at the bar, wearing the same shirt Karl had worn with the big Q in the middle. "Hey Earl, I haven't seen you in a while. What are you up to?"

"I've been doing a lot of studying."

"What are you studying?"

"I joined the Q-Brigade and been reading a lot of their literature. I had no idea of what was going on in this country."

"What did you find out?"

"I learned that Hillary Clinton leads a Satanic cult that drinks chicken blood, and two prominent Senate Democrats practice human sacrifice?"

"I haven't seen any proof of those claims." I picked up my drink and drank it until the glass was empty.

"I read it online, and if it wasn't true, it wouldn't be on the internet."

"You can't trust everything you read on the internet."

"I don't just get my information from the internet. I learn a lot from Twitter too."

Two men walked into the bar and walked up to Earl and asked, "Are you Earl Baker?"

"Yes sir. That's me," Earl replied.

"We'd like to talk to you about the bombing of the Peace Center last week. We need you to come with us."

"Can I at least finish my beer?"

Before finishing his beer, Earl was led out of the bar by the two officers. They put him in the car and took off for the station. Earl had become what we called a Q-Ball, and lucky for us, the FBI was shooting him straight into the side pocket.

Don the Con

I had reached a pinnacle of success I could have never imagined when I was growing up. I was the President of the student government at a school where I was no longer taking classes, and I was making more money than most of the tenured professors. The best part of it was that I had set this up to last for years. I had most of the student body supporting me, even though they had little idea of what I was doing, but as a man much wiser than I once said, what blind people can't see will never offend their sense of vision. Now it was all crashing down on me, and I needed to figure out a way to stay alive.

I was never given a lot of gifts when I was growing up. I looked at my friends, who seemed to get everything. I may not have been given a lot of material things that most kids wanted, but I did get one gift, the gift of gab, and I used it to get whatever I wanted and didn't care who got hurt in the process.

I was fourteen years old when I pulled my first grift. I was talking to Pete Wellington, one of the high school guys who thought he was cooler than a kitchen fan.

"Can you get the stuff or not?" Pete asked.

"Do you have the money?"

"I got it right here." Pete reached into his pocket, pulled out five twenty-dollar bills, and handed them to me. Pete was one of the offensive tackles on the football team and stronger than a mule on steroids.

"I'll be back in about an hour. Where are you going to be?"

"I'll be over by the basketball courts." Then, he asked me one more time, "You sure this stuff is good?"

"You'll be flying," I reassured him. Pete didn't know a bag of weed from a sack of seeds, so I was going to sell him a bag of oregano laced with pot.

I left school and walked a couple of blocks to the supermarket. Walking over to the spice aisle, I bought a large bag of oregano and took it home. I grabbed a baggie and filled eighty percent of it with the oregano and the other twenty percent with some cheap weed I bought from a guy in my building. I gave that to Pete, who thanked me and walked over to his car to get high with a couple of his friends.

When Pete found out he had been sold a bogus bag of weed, he went around school looking for me.

"You got two choices," Pete told me. "Either you give me back my money, or you're gonna wish you did."

"OK. Do you still have the weed?"

"I got a headache and threw it out."

"Wait a minute. If you go to a store and ask for a refund, don't you have to return the merchandise?"

"Yeah."

"What makes you think this is any different? You return the product and I'll return your money."

"I told you, I don't have your product."

"Then I don't have your money. Fair is fair."

"You ripped me off, and now you want to talk about fair?"

"I wasn't the one who ripped you off. My boss made me sell it. I can talk to Rico and see if he'll give you your money back."

"Are you talking about Rico Fortunato?"

"That's right."

"Never mind. He can keep the money."

"Are you sure? I can ask him?"

"No, let him keep the money."

Rico had nothing to do with the bad weed, but Pete didn't know that, and the lie was good enough for Pete to forget about kicking my ass.

I had run a lot of scams after finishing high school and was excited to be lining up my biggest score. One day while walking in Bay Ridge, I ran into Jerry Magadino, whom I had known in high school before he was kicked out for threatening to cripple one of the teachers. Jerry was never going to make the Honor Roll and was too dumb to be stupid. Like more than a few guys in our neighborhood, he dropped out of school and went to work hustling for Rico Fortunato, the neighborhood crime boss.

Jerry always had a lot of money and was the perfect target.

"Jerry, I got a guy down on Wall Street who gives me tips I'm not supposed to get. I've been tripling my money every month.

"How can I get a piece of that?" He took his hands out of his pockets and smiled.

"That depends on how much you want to make."

Jerry scratched his head and asked, "How is this supposed to work?"

"It's simple," I told him. "My guy tells us what stocks to buy, we invest, and then we sell when he tells us the stock is going to tank. We make a killing and only have to give him 5% of our profit."

"And what if this doesn't work?"

"Don't worry. The fix is in. We can't lose."

Over the next month, Jerry gave me three thousand dollars, and as promised, I gave him nine thousand dollars minus the four-fifty kickback to my imaginary partner. Little did he know that I was providing his earnings, but he was so thrilled with what he had made that he was ready to go in big.

A few weeks later, I met Jerry in the back of Peruzzi's deli in Bensonhurst, where he gave me a suitcase filled with hundred dollar bills. It was two hundred thousand dollars. This was going to be my biggest score ever. I was going to keep the money and tell Jerry the scheme got busted by the Feds in an Insider Trading case, and the Feds have his money.

I met Jerry to let him know what was going on.

"Hey Jerry, I got a call from one of my contacts down on Wall Street, and he gave me some bad news."

"What do you mean, bad news?"

"The Feds were conducting this Insider Trading investigation, and my guy got picked up. They froze his trading accounts and put our money on ice."

"Hey Donny, are you fucking kidding me? That wasn't my money. It was Rico's, and if he doesn't get it back, there won't be enough of you and me left to feed the sharks in Sheepshead Bay. We've got three days to come up with his money."

"What does he want me to do? The government took the money. I lost money too, and my friend is probably going to Federal prison."

Rico was the head of a Brooklyn crew that belonged to one of the five mafia families. I wasn't sure whether it was with the Columbo or Gambino family, but at the end of the day, it didn't matter.

"Money's not the only thing you're going to lose. You said the fix was in and we couldn't lose. Now we have to come up with his money or else. How much money can you put together?"

"I don't know. I'm gonna have to get back to you on that."

I had no intention of calling Jerry and giving him any of Rico's money. It was mine. I went to sleep that night dreaming of the things I could buy with the money. I could get a new car or find a new place to live. I felt like good things were about to happen.

About three hours later, while I was asleep, the cold barrel of a gun parted my lips and lodged itself inside my mouth. I opened my eyes and saw Rico Fortunato and two of his crew standing in my apartment. Rico looked more like a businessman than a gangster, wearing a black pin-striped suit and silk tie with a matching handkerchief in his breast pocket. He was smoking a cigar that filled my apartment with an unmistakable odor.

"Get that motherfucker out of the bed," Rico shouted. One of the members of his crew, who was the biggest guy I had ever seen, grabbed me and pulled me to my feet.

"Do you know who I am?" Rico asked.

"Everybody in Brooklyn knows who you are," I replied.

"Then you know I don't fuck around when it comes to my money. I gave your buddy 200K, and he guaranteed I'd triple it. Now you clowns are trying to tell me my money's gone. Well, you got three days to get it back."

"Rico, the money was seized by the Feds. I didn't know that was going to happen. Didn't Jerry tell you?"

"Yeah. He told me right before we dumped his sorry ass in the middle of the Hudson River, and If you don't get me my money, you'll be joining him sooner than you think."

"I can't promise you anything, but I'll see what I can do."

"Well, let me give you a little motivation." He nodded to his associates who started whaling on me like Captain Ahab. First, they punched me in the stomach so hard that I lost my breath. I fell on the floor trying to get air when one of the men kicked the air back into me, doubling the excruciating pain. Then they picked me up again, punching me again and watching me crumble to the floor.

"I don't care how you get my money, but if you don't, there's nowhere in the five boroughs you can hide. I will find you, and you will be dealt with. Did you see how easy it was for us to get in here? It'll be even easier to make you disappear."

Rico dropped some of his cigar ashes on my face and promised they'd be back. I was not looking forward to their visit. Even if I gave Rico his money, they would probably kill me anyway, so I needed to come up with a plan to stay alive.

The only thing I could think of was to get out of town as fast as possible. I went and got the money from a safe deposit box, packed it into a suitcase, and then hustled over to the Port Authority Bus Terminal. I prayed Rico and his crew would not find me before I could get out of town with my life and his money.

I got to Port Authority and bought a bus ticket to Buffalo. If I was on the other side of the State and kept a low profile, it would be hard for Rico to find me. I had enough money to live without working, and I never thought anyone could guess where I had gone. When I got off the bus, I checked into a small hotel until I could find a furnished apartment.

After the first two weeks in the hotel, I bought a copy of the Buffalo News and searched the classifieds for a one-bedroom furnished apartment. I wanted a place close to the Peace Bridge in case I needed to slip into Canada.

I was looking at real estate ads when one caught my attention. It was for a one-bedroom furnished apartment on the top floor of a newly renovated building in walking distance to the Peace Bridge. I took a taxi to the real estate office and met Joan Cheatem, who agreed to show me the apartment.

"Mr. Conway, what do you do for a living?" She asked as we drove over to the apartment.

"My background is in finance."

"Who do you work for?"

"I just moved into town. I haven't found anything suitable yet."

"That could be a problem."

"It's only a problem if you make it one. I have more than enough money to support myself."

"Are you a student?" she asked. "That might be one way around it."

"I was thinking about going back to school and studying finance."

Joan pulled her car in front of a building that reminded me of the nicer buildings on Eastern Parkway. It was six stories with twin gargoyles on the outside of the doorway. We walked inside, took the elevator to the sixth floor, and walked down to the end of the hall. Joan showed me an apartment that was nicely furnished with all new appliances in the kitchen. It had parquet floors and a bathtub that doubled as a jacuzzi. All the rooms were larger than I expected, and I could definitely see myself living there.

Joan and I walked down the hall, and I said, "I really liked the apartment. What do I need to do to make this happen?"

"We might have a problem with you not working. The owner of the building is a stickler for good credit and a steady job."

"I just moved to town. Why should I live in a hotel until I find a job? Plus, having a permanent place to live will help me get a job faster."

"You do make a point," she said. "It's a Catch-22. You can't get a job without a home, and you can't get a home without a job. Either way, I lose."

"How about I fix it so everybody wins?"

"What do you mean?"

"I'll pay you double your usual fee if you get me this apartment. You'll have extra cash, and I'll have a place to live. That's how we both win."

Joan looked at me and smiled. "Make it one and a half times the fee and you've got a deal."

Joan drove me back to my hotel on Delaware Avenue and said she would call me in the morning. I spent the rest of the day trying to figure out what I was going to do once I got settled.

Joan got me the apartment, and I paid her an extra 1,800 dollars on top of the 1,200 I paid her agency. It was three thousand dollars of the money I had swindled from Rico, and as long as I had a nice place to live near the Canadian border, I was OK.

Two weeks after I moved into my apartment, I met Jennifer Osborne, who lived at the other end of the hall. Her light brown hair was neatly trimmed below her neck, and her deep blue eyes sparkled when she smiled. I had seen her a couple of times coming home from school until I ran into her at the supermarket.

I lightly tapped her on the shoulder. "Aren't you my neighbor down the hall?"

She looked at me and replied, "You must be the guy who moved into the Kelly apartment. How do you like it?"

"I love it. My name's Don." I reached out my hand to shake.

She grabbed my hand, shook it, and replied, "I'm Jennifer, but all my friends call me Jen."

"Are you walking home?" I asked.

"I am. Are you heading there too?"

"I am. If you want, I can help you with your groceries."

"You sure it's no trouble?"

"Not at all."

I finished picking up a few things, and after Jen was through with her shopping, we walked down Elmwood Avenue toward our building.

"So, where did you move from?" Jen asked.

"I'm from New York. Brooklyn, to be exact."

"My father used to live in Brooklyn. Have you ever heard of a place called Park Slope?"

"Yeah, I know Park Slope. It's a pretty nice neighborhood."

"He used to live there with the nineteen-year-old girl he left my mother for."

"Does he still live there?"

"No. His girlfriend had a baby, and they moved to Connecticut."

"So, what school do you go to?"

"Buffalo Collegiate."

"Is that a good college? I'm thinking about enrolling in school."

"It's a private high school. I'm a senior there. My mother wants me to move to California with her and go to Stanford."

If she had said she was four years older, I would have believed her. I smiled and looked her up and down, from her eyes to her breasts and then her legs. As someone who got out of high school seven years earlier, I should not have been looking at her that way, but I wondered how far away she was from her eighteenth birthday.

"So you live with your mom?"

"When she's home. My mom's an entertainment lawyer and travels to the West Coast a lot. That's why she wants to move to California."

"What do you want?"

"I just want her to let me make my own decision."

"That sounds like a reasonable thing to ask."

"You should tell her that. She doesn't like listening to me."

We turned off Elmwood Avenue onto Millard and soon walked through the front doors of our building. I helped Jen with the bags all the way to her front door.

She opened the door and said, "It was nice meeting you. I always wondered who moved into that apartment."

"Well now you know," I replied. "And hopefully you won't be a stranger."

I walked down the hall to my apartment and ordered dinner from a Chinese restaurant in the neighborhood.

One month after settling into my apartment, I visited a few used car dealers to buy a car. I was tired of taking the bus and calling cabs, and now that I was getting used to the city, a better mode of transportation was my next order of business.

I ended up buying a light brown Volvo with a dark convertible top. It was in impeccable condition, and I negotiated a great price for cash. That next day I drove my new car home. I obtained my insurance, registered the car, and put new plates on the front and back.

A few days later, I was driving by the local high school and saw Jen walking in the rain without an umbrella. I blew the horn and rolled down the window.

"Hey Jen," I shouted. "Do you need a ride?"

"Are you going home? She asked.

"It looks like today is your lucky day," I told her. She opened the door and jumped into the front seat. As she got into the car, her skirt rose a couple of inches, revealing a beautiful pair of well-developed thighs. I kept one eye on the road while the other focused on the shapely set of legs sitting next to me.

"This is a nice car," she said. "Did you just get it?"

"Yeah, I got tired of taking the bus." We stopped at a light, and I noticed the top two buttons of her blouse were unfastened, revealing the top part of her bra. "If you ever need a ride anywhere, feel free to ask."

"I wouldn't want to inconvenience you. "

"That's what friends are for."

"I won't bother you unless it's an emergency."

I looked at her and smiled. "It can also be for fun. You might be out late one night and need a ride home. You can always call me."

"OK. I'll remember that."

When we got to our building, I took a slip of paper out of the glove compartment and wrote down my phone number. She took the paper and put it in her purse.

That next Friday night I was surprised to get a call from her. She sounded a little upset. "Hey Don, it's Jen. Are you busy?"

"Not really. What's up?"

"I need a favor. I had twenty dollars in my purse, and somehow I lost it and have no way to get home. Could you give me a ride?"

"Of course. Where are you?"

"I'm at the Parkridge Grill, on the corner of Parkside and Jerome."

"I can be there in about fifteen minutes if that's OK?"

"You have no idea how much I appreciate this."

I drove over to the Parkridge Grill, which seemed to be a place where showing proof of age was voluntary. I walked into the place, and except for the bartender, I was the oldest person there. I saw Jen sitting at the end of the bar. I walked over to her, and she gave me a hug and kissed me on the lips. I held her for a couple of seconds before asking. "Are you OK with your tab?"

"Yeah, I'm OK. I just needed to get a ride home, and you were the only person I could think of."

"Even if I was busy, I would have figured out a way to help you."

"I don't know how I can thank you," she said.

"Don't worry about it. Being my friend is enough."

We drove back to the building and took the elevator to the sixth floor.

"You know it's still early," I told her. "Do you feel like coming over and chilling for a while? We could listen to some music, have some beer or wine, and get to know each other."

"That sounds like fun," she smiled as she replied.

In my heart, I knew a twenty-six-year-old man had no business chasing after a high school senior, but at that time I didn't care.

Jen sat down in the middle of the couch while I put on the radio and poured two glasses of wine. I handed one to her and sat down on the couch.

She took a sip of the wine, put her hand on my leg, and said, "Thanks for coming to get me."

I grabbed her hand and said, "C'mon, you know I've got your back. I've got a question. Do you smoke?"

"You have some weed?"

"Yeah, I've got some great stuff. Let me roll a joint." I walked into my bedroom, took a bag of Acapulco Gold out of my dresser, and rolled a fat joint. I lit it and handed it to her.

"Wow, this stuff is good." She took another couple of hits and gave the joint back to me.

I took one more hit and put it in the ashtray. I moved closer to Jen, putting my hand on her leg, and said, "This is the best time I've had in a long time."

We looked into each other's eyes and started making out. First it was kissing. Then as we got more intense, I unfasted two buttons of her blouse and reached my hand around her back to unfasten the latch of her bra. Next, I started licking her nipples and kissing her body, working my way down.

We woke up the next day in my bed, naked in each other's arms, before taking a shower together.

Jen and I maintained our relationship without her mother ever suspecting anything. We were very careful when we went out. Sometimes I would drop her off down the street so no one would see us hanging out too often. If anyone had ever told her mother or called the authorities, I would be facing some serious legal exposure.

I took Joan Cheatem's suggestion and registered to take a class in Finance at Naldon University. I was still holding the cash I had swindled from Rico, which I stashed in another safe deposit box, and figured I might as well learn how to invest it and make it grow.

Walking through the student union one day, I heard two people debating why they should be elected to run the student government. They argued about managing the budget and renegotiating contracts with vendors who wanted the school's business.

The debaters argued about how they would improve things, but no one seemed to be connecting with the people listening. As boring as they were, I knew I could do better. It was at that moment my collegiate political career was launched. I went to the student government office and picked up some information on their duties and responsibilities. They controlled a budget of thirty-two million dollars and were responsible for all the cultural activities taking place on campus. They were funded by student fees, and if the Board thought they were having a shortfall, they would just raise the student fees. I would have control of money that would probably not be monitored very closely. If I could get that job, I might never have to work.

The first thing I had to do to run for the position was to get the signatures of one hundred students to qualify for the ballot. I spent the next few days getting my signatures and planning my campaign. I needed to do something to help me stand out from everybody else. This could be a dream come true. In my first semester in college, I was already running for President. I didn't know anything about running student government, but how hard could it be? You run things the way you like and get other people to do the work.

I went home and started thinking about how I could generate some excitement at my rallies so they wouldn't be like the corny ones I saw from the other candidates. I wanted to have loud music and scantily clad dancing girls.

I called Jen and asked if she could come by the apartment.

"Thanks for coming by," I told her.

"What's up?"

"I need your help."

"What do you need?"

"I'm running for student government and need some help with my rallies. I'm willing to pay for the help."

"What do you want me to do?"

"I need some dancers to entertain people before I come out and speak. I'd be willing to pay you and four of your friends to dance and campaign with me. We'll do three or four rallies, and I might want you guys to help me pass out some flyers."

"I can't ask my friends to skip class."

"All the rallies will be in the late afternoon or early evening. It won't interfere with your school, and you guys will pocket some nice cash."

"Just let me know when you want to get started."

"I knew I could count on you. I reached over and kissed her. She kissed me back, and I slipped my hand under her blouse. "What time do you have to get home?"

"My mom is flying in on the redeye, so I have some time." That was all I needed to hear before we started taking our clothes off, leaving them in a pile in the middle of the floor. I carried her into the bedroom, put her down on the edge of the bed, and crawled on top. We had sex for the next hour and a half before she got dressed and went home.

If I invested a thousand dollars in the campaign and won, I could control a budget of over thirty million dollars. This was worth every penny I was paying Jen and her friends. If I played my cards right, I could be living in Grifter's Paradise.

I used the Rolling Stones' *Gimme Shelter* as my theme song, and I always ended my rallies with *You Can't Always Get What You Want*. It was played loud and attracted people's attention. The girls came out initially in robes dancing to the music, then pulled the robes off in a burlesque-style movement and danced in skimpy bikinis. The men in the audience loved it, while some of the ladies weren't impressed. I didn't care because I was stirring up the excitement.

While I was running for office, my platform was lowering tuition, reducing student fees, and providing more quality free entertainment. That was the platform I was standing on.

News of my campaign quickly spread all over the campus. The school newspapers had editorials for and against me, and to tell you the truth, I didn't care either way. As long as they were talking about me, it was working to my advantage. Some people questioned how I was going to implement my policy objectives, but I never gave them a straight answer. I always replied that I didn't want to give my competitors any ideas. If they wanted to know how I would implement things, they had to elect me first.

I even got Jen to plant another one of her friends in the crowd to ask me softball questions. We used that in case someone started asking me too many questions for which I didn't have the answers. I paid her too, but not as much as the dancers.

By the time we were doing the last rally. The race was coming down to me and a woman named Marie Godwin. She was a Dean's List student who had served in many different capacities in the student government and challenged me to a debate. Though I didn't want to do the debate, backing out could sway the election against me. So when we set the ground rules for the evening, I insisted that my group be allowed to entertain the audience before the debate. This was non-negotiable. Eventually, they relented and agreed to let my dancers do their thing.

My dancers did their usual semi-burlesque show behind the blaring music.

The moderator asked me the first question. "Mr. Conway. You said you want to reduce student fees and eliminate high-ticket costs for top quality entertainment. How do you plan to do that?"

I looked up at her and replied, "It's easy. The people who were running the student government before didn't know what they were doing and had no idea of how to negotiate good deals. I want to negotiate better deals, eliminate the middlemen and pass the savings back to you, the students. When my opponent was part of the student government, she made some of those bad deals. It's time someone put the students first, and that's what I plan to do."

A tremendous roar came from the crowd, and I could hear them chanting the name Conway over and over.

The last question the moderator asked was how I could run a large fiscal budget when I didn't have any experience managing a complex organization.

"Running a government means you're the head of the team, not the entire team. You have to put the right people in place and make them accountable for succeeding. Being the head of a company doesn't mean you have to know every job in the company."

The next week, when all the votes were tallied, I won by one of the widest margins ever. Now I had to learn how to govern the student body of a school I had only attended for a few weeks.

For the next few weeks, I read everything I could about student government. After the first meeting of the Executive Team, I figured out who I could trust and who I needed to get rid of.

I looked over the financial records but had no idea what anything meant, so I hired one of my friends from my finance class to explain it to me. I made a deal to pay him as a consultant out of the organization's budget. I recruited two other classmates to analyze the entertainment expenditures and prepare a report on which contracts were expiring this year.

I was never going to reduce student fees. That was campaign talk. I told everyone I heard there was talk of doubling student fees, but after I threatened a boycott, the fees would be frozen for the next two years. There was no truth to this, but why mess up a good story?

I was getting so involved with my work as the head of the student government that I didn't have any time left to go to class. The semester was coming to an end, and unless I did something, I would have to run for office again.

I thought I could solidify my hold on power if we had a referendum, giving people the opportunity to voice their opinions on matters important to them. One of the things people voted for was the elimination of one-year terms. I argued that In order to get more done for the students, the government needed continuity, and indeterminant length terms were the only way we could do it. The students voted to approve this, so now I wouldn't have to run for re-election. This school business was better than any scam I had ever pulled in New York.

After my first month in office, I met everyone who had a contract to provide entertainment for us. This was especially true if they had an expiring agreement and wanted to continue working with us. I asked every vendor who wanted to do business with the student government to make a donation to the charity of my choice. My finance team set up the charity where the money was funneled. We were making tens of thousands a month, and it was all ours. We took that money, invested it in the market, and put our profits in offshore accounts.

Pretty soon, I spent less time governing and more of it shaking down vendors who wanted to keep doing business with the school. I never thought government could be so good. I might stay here for life with no term limits on this position.

For the next six months, we worked the skim to perfection. We were taking our cut from the vendors, investing it, and moving the profits out of the country.

Unfortunately, like all good things, this too would come to an end. Two vendors complained about having to contribute to my charity, which prompted an investigation. Forensic accountants went over our books and asked us to account for the money. Because we had managed to keep the principal, our attorneys offered to return the fake charity money. I still kept the capital gains and interest, which was substantial. The returned principal and $45,000 in legal fees kept me out of jail. The school asked that I withdraw from the university and agree to never run for student government again. I agreed, but still walked away with thousands of dollars parked in numbered accounts out of the country.

Jen called and said she needed to talk to me. We agreed to meet after she got home from school. I told her I'd order some pizza and pick up some beer. When she got to my place, I was still trying to figure out why we needed to talk.

"What's going on?" I asked.

"My period is late," she said.

"Do you think you're pregnant?"

"I don't know."

"Who do you think the father might be?"

"You're the only person I've been with in the last eight months."

"Do you want me to pay for the abortion?"

"I'm not sure that's what I want to do. I might want to keep the baby."

"Do you think that's a good idea? What about your education?"

"I wouldn't be the first woman attending school after having a baby."

"What about me? I'm not looking to be held down by a family."

"I thought you loved me."

"I do, but maybe it's time we stop seeing each other."

"Why?" she said, as tears started running down her face.

"This is not my permanent home, and I could leave anytime. I don't want anything holding me down. You and a baby would not be in my best interests right now."

_n got up, left, and didn't call me again. If this was our breakup, I was ready to move on.

Two weeks after our breakup, I got a knock on my door. I opened it and saw two police officers with a paper in one of their hands.

"Are you Don Conway? The officer asked.

"Yes."

"We have a warrant for your arrest."

"What for? I haven't done anything."

"Do you know a woman named Jennifer Osborne?"

"Yes. She's my neighbor."

"You're being charged with statutory rape and contributing to the delinquency of a minor."

"Jen is accusing me of raping her?"

"No, she isn't. Her mother filed the complaint and Jennifer corroborated everything. Can you put your hands behind your back?"

I was taken to the Erie County jail to wait until my trial. Two days after I was arrested, I was on my way to dinner when one of the inmates walked up to me.

"Are you Don Conway?" he asked.

"Who wants to know?"

"Rico sends his regards and says you'll be hearing from him real soon."

Made in the USA
Middletown, DE
24 June 2023

33330878R00137